Drew

JUSTICE SERIES BOOK 5

KATHI S. BARTON

This is a work of fiction. Names, characters, places, and incidents are products of the author's imagination or are used fictitiously and are not to be construed as real. Any resemblance to actual events, locations, organizations, or persons, living or dead, is entirely coincidental.

World Castle Publishing, LLC
Pensacola, Florida
Copyright © Kathi S. Barton 2016
Paperback ISBN: 9781629895840
eBook ISBN: 9781629895857
First Edition World Castle Publishing, LLC, November 14, 2016
http://www.worldcastlepublishing.com
Licensing Notes
Cover: Karen Fuller
Editor: Maxine Bringenberg

CHAPTER 1

Addie put the phone back on the hook and sat down. Since she'd gotten up she'd been trying to reach out to her friend, Mac, and hadn't gotten a single answer, or a call back when she left her messages. She was coming here in a few days to hang out with her and to meet her new friends. But now, trying to get in touch with Mac and not having any success made her worry. Something was wrong, she just knew it. Going to find Nick, she wasn't surprised to find Landon and Steele in the office with him. Nick stood up when she entered the room and gave her his seat. The man was a constant worrywart, especially since she'd found out she was expecting. She wasn't sure she could make it the next few months without bashing his head in.

"Here, honey, please have a seat. And put your feet up on the stool. Did you get in touch with her?" Addie told him that she'd not as she sat down in his chair, but she didn't put her feet up. There was only so much pampering she could take right now. "I know that you're worried. I think you need to call her place of business. Didn't you tell me she works for some sort of boating company?"

"Extreme. And she doesn't just work for them, but owns

5

the company, though few people know that. I'm pretty sure not even the people that work for her are aware of it, believing they just work with her. But, no, I've not called yet. I wanted to ask you first. I don't want her to think I'm overprotective of her. She accused me of that in college when we were younger." Addie rubbed her growing belly as she continued. "It's not like her to not call me back. I know that it's silly, but I'm afraid something has happened to her. But I don't want to feel stupid for calling her work and embarrassing her. Do you understand?"

"Call them." When Steele nodded in agreement with Nick, she thought she'd do it. But later. "No, not later, now. Call them and ask where she is. You know that you're not sleeping well worrying over this. She will get a good laugh out of it and so will you, but you won't worry anymore. Just go ahead and call and see what might be going on. It might be something simple, like her phone is down or something like that."

Getting up, she went to her own office. If she was going to feel stupid for calling for no reason other than Mac was really busy, she'd rather do it where no one could hear her. Picking up the phone and dialing the number she'd memorized yesterday, she wasn't surprised when the answering machine picked up. But she was no less worried either.

"Hello. You're going to think this is really silly, but I'm trying to get in touch with Ryder Mackenzie. Mac. She goes by Mac. Anyway, my name is Addie Stark and she was supposed to call me back and—"

"Hello? Don't hang up. Please, just hang on while I try to turn this off." The woman, she thought it was Sandy Miller who worked for Mac, cursed a few times as buttons were pushed. "I'm not very good at this thing. Mac usually...please call back if I hang up on us."

After telling the woman that she would, the line went dead. Addie sat there for several minutes trying to reason with her fingers to dial the numbers again when it rang. Picking up the phone carefully, she heard more cursing and knew it was Sandy again.

"I'm so sorry. I'm not the office type. Cameras yes, but...I just came in here to pick up the money and heard you. There's nobody around to help me out on this thing." Addie told her it was all right. "Mac is...She's in the hospital, has been since late yesterday. Mac is...I mean she...they don't really expect her to make it. She took a terrible tumble over the falls near where she lives, and...and...poor baby...."

The sobbing was what got her. The woman was sobbing so hard that it sounded as if she were tearing her heart out. Addie felt her own eyes fill with tears, then run over as she thought of her friend lying dead. Mac was such a vibrant and full of life woman. Knowing that she was hurt and might not make it...well, Addie knew that she'd feel it forever if she were to pass. Her sorrow became more as Sandy told her what she knew.

"She told me she was going home, and I never thought anymore about it until I heard the scanner going off and her telling them that she had three in the water. A little kid, she said. They didn't have any life jackets on them, so...oh, that poor little thing. I turned the cameras around to find her and saw it. Just saw that kayak go right over with her hanging onto that child. I think there was some man trying to help her save the girl, but...well, he died too. Mac said that...she said that she was going after her. I knew as soon as I heard there was a little one involved that she'd go and try to save her. But those falls, even for someone experienced like her, they're a

7

bit much, especially this time of year. She and that little girl went right over, and I never saw them again until I made my way to the hospital." Addie was crying hard now, knowing that Mac would hurt herself to save anyone, but especially a little kid. As the story unfolded, Addie could almost see it happening. "Those people on the raft, they were all screaming at the police when they got there. Took them a good five minutes to get them calmed down enough to tell them where she'd gone over. By then…well, it was damned near too late for all of them."

"The child, is she all right?" Sandy said that she was broken up pretty good, but was expected to make a full recovery. "And the others, what happened to them?"

"Both parents are gone. The mister, Adam was his name, he broke his neck. They think he might have been dead before he ended up on the bottom of the falls, but we don't know for sure. His wife, Cindy, little Becky's mother, she drowned. Again, they don't know for sure when that happened. Like I said, the falls are unforgiving if you don't know how to run them." Addie wanted to ask about Mac's injuries, but was afraid to. But Sandy spoke before she could. "Mac was beaten up, near dead when they got to her. Her head was split open by the rocks, and they're worried about what sort of damage…they're worried about brain damage. Broke both her arms and crushed her leg. The doctor told me that she'd be lucky if she walked again without a cane. Then he broke down. Imagine that, a doctor breaking down, and he told me that she wasn't going to live out the night, not the way she was right now. That was…she's my little girl and she's been hanging on since. They had to…I won't let them just let her go. She'll never forgive me for doing that. She's not one to hang on, she told me more than once. But they brought her

8

back for us. The staff there at the critical care, they don't...I don't know what I'm supposed to do without her. She's all I have...I love her like my own."

"I'm coming there." Addie stood up, then sat down when she thought of what she had to do. "I'll be there in the morning, if not tonight. Can you find a place for me to stay? Please? I need to be there for her."

"Oh honey, that would be wonderful for us. Me too. Yes, that's good. Yes, of course you need to be here. And I'd like that too. She talked of nothing else but seeing you. It's why I picked up the machine. And you come on out here. You can stay in her place if you want. It's a big place, but she loves it. That pup of hers will be more than glad to see someone besides me." Addie wasn't sure about a puppy. All she cared about right now was seeing her friend and maybe trying to figure out a way to bring her around. "I'll have someone pick you up at the hangar. Not much of an airport, but we make do."

Addie hung up a few minutes later after taking notes on not only where to go but how to get to the house if she ended up staying there. Still not sure what she was going to do once she got there, Addie went to find Nick. She was leaving right now if she could arrange it.

~~~

Drew wandered around the house again, ending up near his own room. He wasn't sure yet what he was supposed to do with his new house, but he thought he was making headway. The house was so big that at times he felt smothered by it. Stupid he supposed, but that was the feeling he got. And if he was honest with himself, he wasn't sure he liked this place. It was...dark, he thought was a good word for it. Dark and not suited to him at all.

Anna, his cook, and right now the only person he saw much of, was in the kitchen for the most part while he was there, and he'd finally convinced her to stay in the pool house instead of driving back and forth every day. Most days they both ate in the kitchen, as he just couldn't stand the thought of her carrying what food she thought was good for him between the dining room and the kitchen like he was something special. Smiling at that thought, he went out onto the deck that was off his bedroom.

It was the one thing he'd loved about the house. The way the deck, all covered and filled with the most comfortable furniture, seemed to invite a person to come and have a seat. To kick off their shoes, as he had done when he'd sat down, and relax. He wondered if the previous owners of the house, Landon's parents, had ever had an occasion to relax at all between stealing from people and making everyone's life hard.

He supposed that he should have taken the master suite when he moved in, but it was bigger by far than one floor of his other home. Not to mention he had yet to go through the personal things in the room, and Landon had told him there was nothing there he wanted of his parents. He guessed he could hire someone to do it, but he had no idea how to even begin that task. Putting his feet up on the stool that matched the rest of the furniture, he looked out over the wooded area behind his house.

The deer came out about now, and he'd made it a habit when he was home to watch them. It was relaxing, and he never thought much when he watched them romp and play. Yesterday there had been a small one with them, and he had enjoyed watching it get its feet under it. The buck, a big boy with about a dozen points, just watched him. Drew wondered if he'd learn to trust him soon.

"Drew?" He looked up at the sound of his name, afraid, not for the first time since he'd moved in when he heard his name in such an unfamiliar place. Instead of being his mother coming to haunt him again, it was Anna. "Are you all right, sir? I didn't mean to startle you like that. I said your name a couple of times."

"It's fine. My fault entirely. I'm all right, I promise. You just...I was surprised, that's all. What is it I can do for you?" She looked out over the woods then back at him. He knew that she thought him a little off. If she only knew how off he really was, she'd more than likely go running into the woods to get away from him. "I was watching the family of deer that come around. They have a way of making even the worst day nicer with their ways, don't you think?"

"Yes, I think so as well. I saw them as well two nights ago, and slept better knowing they were here for some reason." He waited for her to continue, and thought perhaps she was telling him she was quitting. "There's someone here to see you. Miss Vinnie and Miss Addie. They're in the parlor. I told them you'd be along shortly. I can tell them you need a few moments if you'd like."

"No, I'll come along now. Thank you. And if you have any cookies, I know that Addie loves them." She blushed and told him she had some, and some scones too if she was of a mind to try them. "I'm sure that she'd love that. Thank you." Drew knew that Anna was aware of what they all were. Vinnie was a vampire, and Kari, Steele's wife, was a panther shifter. Then there were the rest of them, all necromancers with a little extra that came in handy when they worked.

As he made his way to the big room, he wondered what they needed. Right now he'd do just about anything to stem

11

the boredom. He'd never been one to sit idle, because the memories invaded even his waking thoughts. And since he was off for the rest of the week, he had to find something to do or go nuts…well, nuttier. Entering the room, he smiled at them as if he had not a care in the world.

Addie was adorable with her belly starting to show. She was about four months now, and he could see that she was extremely happy. So was Nick. All he ever talked about was the new baby. Drew was sort of jealous of him getting that experience, as he knew that he never would.

"Ladies, have you come to help me figure out the house? I sure could…. What's happened?" He could tell by their faces that something was wrong, and he immediately thought of the men that he worked with. He sat down when Vinnie stared to pace. Whatever it was, it wasn't going to be good.

"Nick is going away on a call, as I'm sure you know, and we're in sort of a pickle. I've always wanted to use that phrase. Anyway, we need your help." He nodded at Addie, knowing from the call this morning that the others were going to be awhile. And they wouldn't let him go with them. It was a new rotation thing they were doing, so that they could spend more time with families and not be so burnt out all the time. One week off, two on was how it had been set up. Drew hated it.

"There's been an accident with a friend of Addie's. She needs to go there and…it's not good." Drew asked Vinnie what he could do. "I can watch over her in the evenings, but the day time, I can't as you well know. Can you come with us? Nick said that he'd prefer we both went rather than her be alone during the day."

"You know I'll do anything for you guys." He would, too. "When do you want to leave? I'm assuming now. All I need to do is throw a few things into a bag and I'm set."

"Yes, that would be wonderful. We have the plane on standby. I don't know how long we'll be gone...my friend, Mac, she was hurt pretty bad when her kayak went over the falls while she was...while she was trying to rescue a little girl. She...the little girl's parents drowned and...I need to be with her; Mac, not the child."

"I'll go and pack now." He stood up and then moved to the door just as Anna was coming in with a tray of cookies and tea. Drew asked them to let her know what was going on as he left to pack.

Tossing things into his duffel bag, he thought of the friendship that he had with these people. All of them were family, and he'd do just about anything they asked when they needed him. He didn't share most of the things going on in his life as they did. He trusted them, but not with knowing his secret. It was bad enough that he'd had to live through what his mother had done to him; he didn't think he could stand to see their pity when they looked at him. Drew had always been a very private person, and it hadn't changed much when he became an adult.

He wondered if they thought of him as a friend, as someone they could trust, and believed perhaps they did. He worked with the men on the team, and he liked them a great deal. But he was a loner. He didn't like it very much, but it was all he knew. Keeping busy was what kept him from thinking, and thinking was a dangerous thing for him. His childhood, his life, had made him that way. He'd always been alone, and deterred people from asking too many questions. Questions that Drew didn't want to answer.

Then there was the added fact that he was scarred. Not just in his mind, but his body as well. Badly. The worst of them were mostly on his back and the back of his legs; the ones on his torso were faded, as they hadn't been nearly as bad. It was what caused him so much pain when he got up in the morning or after standing or sitting in one position for too long. And long ago he knew that if he didn't kick the pain pills he'd be as drugged up as his mother had been most of her life. Drew didn't want to end his life that way. So now, he simply suffered.

Andrew? His entire body stiffened at the sound of the voice. It was distant, but he knew it anyway. Turning slowly around the room, he looked for his mother, only to find himself alone in the big bedroom. But he knew as surely as he was standing there, she was close. *Andrew, where the hell are you, boy?*

Not answering her seemed the best way to keep her at bay. Stuffing the rest of his things in his bag, he tried to think what he had to do to rid himself of her if she found him again. The need to have her banished, kept away from him, nearly took him to his knees. Even after all she'd done to him and continued to do, she was still his mother. But even as he zipped up the bag and headed out, he knew he was never going to be able to make his mother go away forever. Because he was still that ten-year-old little boy.

"Are you ready?" Telling Vinnie that he was, she looked at him oddly. He wondered if she could see his mother, or if any of them could, and that made him feel exposed. He hadn't thought they could, but with Vinnie, who knew? And he was hard pressed to ask her if she could or not. But Vinnie only turned and went to his front door, met there by Anna. Drew thought about asking Vinnie for help with his mom, but didn't. Fear and pride made him keep his mouth shut.

"I packed some cookies and tea for the trip. I know that your plane must have all these things, but I worry so about you." Anna gave him the large plastic container, filled to the top with cookies and wrapped scones, and the thermos of tea. "Sugar is there, as well as cream if you need it. Not sure how the rest of you take your tea."

After she hugged Addie and Vinnie and left them, Drew went to the big car that Addie and Nick had only just recently purchased. Since she handed him the keys, he put his bag in the back of it with the other two pieces of luggage and got in the driver's seat. Just as he was ready to start it up to go, his cell phone rang. It was Nick.

"Thank you for doing this for me." He told him it was no problem, he was glad to help out. "She's really stressed out about this. If she...this woman, I guess she's really bad off. I had a couple of the guys here go and check on her, and Addie is going to be devastated when she sees her. I guess they were right in saying she might not make it."

"Addie told me that the secretary said that they didn't expect her to make it past the first night. Perhaps her hanging on this way is a good sign." Addie got in the back with Vinnie. It was darker back there, because even though it was nearly evening, the sun still burned Vinnie a little. Being a vampire had some difficult rules attached to it. "The little girl's parents, should I be looking for them there? I mean, they might want to hang out with their daughter for a little while."

"I never thought of that. But I would keep an eye out for them. I don't know what sort of people they were alive, but we both know that things change when they figure out they're dead. The little girl is in a deep coma, but I'm not sure if it's drug induced or just from all the injuries. She is only alive because of Addie's friend, I guess. They have her head cam and it shows pretty much everything that happened to the two of them when they went over the falls." Drew wondered if Addie would want to see that, and thought she might be better off if she didn't. It had to be pretty horrific. "Anyway, I want you to call me if you need anything. Steele got you guys a nice hotel, and I guess Vinnie has a place she can stay while out there too. There is the woman's house too. There is a dog; I'm not sure what it is, but he'll need some looking over too. I can't thank you guys enough for helping me out."

"I'm glad to have something to do, to be honest." He put the phone on the holder and stuck his earphones in. One thing he did not do was drive and hold onto his phone at the same time. He wouldn't even answer it until he pulled over to do so. Drew might not like his life overly much, but he'd not take out others just to end his. "Is there anything else I might need to know out there? I mean for Addie. She's pretty upset."

"Not that I know of. She's been talking about this girl for a while now. They've met at least once a year since they got out of college. Her family is gone, so I think she might only have the people she works with. She owns this company, Extreme. There are several of them across the United States, so I think she's done well for herself." Drew was impressed with that. Not that as a woman she'd done well, but that she wasn't any older than Addie and was successful. "She's also somewhat of a loner. Not like you, but pretty close. If she's not working, then she's at home. And Addie wanted me to see if you'd take care of the dog. Again, I'm not sure what kind it is, but Sandy, the woman who works for Mac, said he's all right. Addie didn't feel right staying at her house. She said it would be too painful."

"I'll take care of it. And you know I love being alone." He knew that he'd sounded defensive, but Nick only laughed. "I'll let you know when we get there. And I'll take care of the dog too."

"Like I said, I really appreciate this. And should this girl pass, I'll drop everything here and make it out. I've already made some arrangements with Steele." Drew told him he'd replace him. "Thanks for doing this for me. For us. Hopefully it will turn out all right for everyone."

In Drew's experience it rarely turned out well. Most of the time, if it could go to shit for him, it did. He ended the call and drove to the airport. Everything was set, and they were up in the air within twenty minutes of getting everything stowed away.

Drew thought about what he had now compared to what he'd had as a kid. Since working for Steele, he now had a car, credit cards for company trips, and a home. Money to spend should he do so carefully. Enough clothing that he was warm when needed. A television that didn't only work when it wanted to, and ample food in the house that he was never hungry.

Shirts and pants, dressy when needed or casual when working, were also provided. His personal items—socks, shoes, and other items such as underwear and tees—were his own to buy, and he rarely spent much on those. And now, thanks to Landon and his wife, he had a house bigger than he needed, and servants too. He still wasn't sure what to do with all that, but it was his, and no one else's.

Closing his eyes for the trip, Drew felt himself drift off. As his body relaxed, his mind became fertile. His mother was just there, memories of her fighting with his need to vanquish her from his mind. As he drifted deeper into sleep, his mother was welcoming him to her horror.

"Do you have any idea how much I despise you right now?" The ten-year old Drew whimpered. "Shut up. Just shut up. If I could afford it, I'd end you right now and be done with you."

17

He never answered her; to speak to her when she was stoned, as she had been, would have been bad. To have done so would have given her another reason to hurt him. And she did enough of that without his help. Instead, he sat there on the floor with his towel under his body, so the blood from his latest injuries wouldn't ruin the carpet beneath him. His mother wanted to make sure they made a good impression when the welfare people came by to check on him. They did it less and less as he had gotten older, and he doubted very much that any of them cared what sort of state the house was in so long as he was there and still breathing.

She didn't love him. He'd figured that out long ago. And even if he hadn't figured it out, it wouldn't have mattered. She told him almost hourly how much she despised him. He was her means to get what she wanted, whatever that was. Her anger at him was legendary. But this time, she was madder than he'd ever seen her. And getting angrier by the second.

He was sure she'd broken his nose. His jaw, on a previous beating, had been bruised badly, but not broken. Now it was painful to move, even if he did want to speak to her. Drew looked at her when she screamed his name.

"Pay attention to me, you moron. Or so help me, I'm going to teach you a lesson you won't ever forget. No one will look at you with pity again, by God." She had hit him then, his arms tied above his head to her canopy bed. Pain made him sick, dizzy even, as he had no way of getting down. Not until she let him, cutting at the ropes until he just simply dropped to the floor.

Drew had hung there before, more times than he wanted to remember. She would tie him there, beat him over a couple of days, then let him down, telling him how it had been his fault that she'd been driven to beat him. Again.

18

As he had drifted off, his entire being worn out, his adult mind tried to tell him to get away, to run, to hide. But it did him no good; what was to come was coming no matter what he did now, even if he could have gotten away.

"Drew?"

His name, said so softly, startled him. The dream, the memory really, had him in its clutches tightly, and he knew she was coming for him. As soon as he was touched, a small hand to his shoulder, Drew fought, lashed out at whoever was trying to hurt him. When he realized that he'd been dreaming and that his mother wasn't there, Drew knew that he'd made a major mistake.

Staring down at the face under him, Drew tried to think what had happened. How Vinnie had a bloodied mouth, her lip already swelling. Her hands were above her head, palms out. She didn't move, said nothing as they lay there. It was the voice behind him that had him knowing he'd fucked up, and had done something terrible. He was going to have to explain what he'd done, as if he even knew how to.

"Drew, are you okay?" Was he? No. And would never be if he didn't get over this fear of his mother. "Drew, please answer me and let Vinnie breathe. I'm scared that you're hurting her."

His hands were curled around her throat. The bruising there was already making itself known to him. Letting go, his fingers loosening even as the grip of the memories did, he felt his heart twist, and his mind begin to work. Fear slid over him as a shirt did when he was fresh from his shower.

"I'm so sorry." Sliding his heavier body off hers, he lay there, curling his body into a fetal position and trying to wrap his mind around what he had just done. "I had a bad dream. I'm so sorry. I never meant to hurt you. I'm very sorry."

19

"Who is she?" He thought of his mother when Vinnie asked him the question. He wasn't even aware he'd answered her aloud until she spoke again. "Is your mother dead, Drew? Does she haunt you even now? Is she the person that you were thinking about when you came into the living room today?"

"It was her. She never leaves me alone. But yes, she's dead. And does she haunt me?" He laughed bitterly, knowing that he would have to tell her in order to make up for what he'd done. "Every waking moment of my life, even when I'm not asleep."

Drew didn't know how long he lay there. He knew that they had landed, the vibration of the engines running now gone. The women spoke quietly, but still he didn't move. The need to get up, run, and hide had him fighting for some sort of control over himself.

After a while, when he knew he couldn't put it off any longer, he sat up and stared at them. Not sure what he needed to say, he opened his mouth, hoping for something brilliant, when Addie spoke first.

"It's really late, so Vinnie will be with me now. Why don't you go to the house, Mac's house, and see to her puppy and rest? I heard you tell Nick you'd help with that. Then in the morning, you can bring me breakfast and hang out with me. Okay?" Drew nodded and waited for either of them to ask questions. When they both stood and went to the exit, he let out a long breath. He didn't think he was off the hook, but he did buy himself some much needed time.

Taking a cab to the address given to him by Addie, Drew knew a new kind of fear. They knew he was haunted, and worse yet, by whom. He wondered what they were going to tell the others, knowing that they would. Drew also wondered which one of them would call him first and tell him he was fucking nuts.

20

CHAPTER 2

Aster knew that Addie was resting when she started to enter the room. There was a calmness about her that always made her feel good. But the voices, or one voice, had her pausing before she moved into the room so that she could be seen by anyone there. The man's voice, full of anger and hate, had her reaching for her grandda. She had no idea what to expect, but the other man's voice finally became clear enough for her to understand, and she faded into the room with her temper high.

"What do you think you're doing?" The man looked around the room as if he wasn't sure she was talking to him. "You. What are you doing talking to her that way? You have no right to tell her to die when there are others here that want to see her live."

"I can do whatever the fuck I want to do. She fucking killed me." Aster looked at the woman on the bed then back at the man. "You know her? If you do, then you have to come here and help me kill her off. She owes me for not saving me first. She just moved by me like I wasn't there, and that just ain't right. I don't deserve to be dead, but she does."

"No one deserves to be dead the way you were killed. But I doubt very much it was her fault. You're the little girl's

21

father, aren't you?" He nodded and glared at her. "I'd think you'd be happy that your child lived. And that this woman saved her. Not standing over her telling her that she has nothing left to live for and—"

"She should have saved me first. And then my wife if there was time. Not necessary, I guess, but I should have been saved. We all would have lived had she just come to me instead of going after my kid. Do you know what we could have done if we had worked together?" He looked down at Mac then back at her. "That woman fucked me over by going after my kid first and saving her useless ass. Now what the hell am I supposed to do? I'm dead."

"You're not thinking about this right. She was able to save your child. Had she moved to you first, your little girl would have gone over the falls alone and died. You surely didn't want that, did you?" The man said nothing. "And your wife. What does she think of this?"

"I have no idea. I can't drag her away from the kid's bedside. Sits there all day and night just watching over her like she can do a damned thing about anything that happens to her. Why she even cares is beyond me. Cindy was forever putting the needs of that kid before mine." He leaned down to Mac's ear again. "Die, you fucking cunt. Die so that when you come to this side, I can show you the real meaning of pain."

"Stop that." The monitors over the bed started to beep, and before long, Aster knew that they'd start screaming that she was in some distress. Going to the other side of the bed, Aster put her hand over Mac's heart and sent her some of her energy. Not a great deal, but enough to get the monitors to slow. Turning to the man she knew was going to be major trouble, she pushed a little more of her energy and anger at him. "Get out of here before I call on my family to come and banish you. Mean spirited people such as yourself aren't welcome here."

"Like I give a shit. She murdered me as surely as if she had held me under the water with her bare hands. Then if that wasn't enough, I broke my neck, so that had I even been able to live through this shit, I wouldn't have been able to get around on my own. That's just not fucking right, is it?" Aster started to tell him he was wrong but he snarled at her, much like a dog would, and left her. Aster looked down at the woman, nearly broken by what she'd done to save the child.

"You won't die, no matter what he's said to you. Addie needs you, as do we all. And so does Drew. He will need you most of all." Aster turned to look at Addie, then back at Mac. "She will help you as well when you wake. The powers that you now have, the reason you must live, will help them all because of what you do for him. You will live, Ryder Mackenzie. There is someone here that needs you very badly. He's not even aware of it as yet."

Aster watched Mac. The monitors were now quiet, with only the small beep-beep that said that her heart was beating, as well as the one that helped her breathe. Aster knew that she could help her with that. She'd done so before, but she waited until she was needed again. Mac had to live. So much depended on it.

When her grandda entered the room, he asked her if she was all right. "I am now. Thank you for coming so quickly. We need to keep better care over this one. The man that died when she saved his daughter is trying to harm her. He wants her to die so that he can be monstrous to her on the other side. I wonder if he thinks it will really work that way. She'd be stronger than him anyway, right?" He nodded and told her that the mean had powers, but the good, they had them better.

"She can't die, Grandda. As you know, Drew really does need her."

"I know, child. I know. The mother, have you gone to see her yet?" She asked him which one, Drew's or the little girl's. "The child's. There is no talking to the other. She's got it in her head that she's still alive and will not listen to reason. I don't understand why.... Well, Drew will be all right if this one lives, I think. But we're going to end up doing something about that Belinda, Drew's mother. There's a fine piece of work if I ever done did see one. Nasty woman. And the way she treated that boy of hers. Had I known? Well, I'm telling you, things would have been a lot different. For both of them."

"None of us knew anything. He's been so quiet about his life and his mother. To think that he kept this all inside of him for all this time. I think she might be worse than my mother was with Steele and me." Aster nodded as she continued. "Grandda, how did you know that Mac was Drew's other half? I mean...you didn't plan this, did you? The accident, I mean?"

"Oh no. No, never that. But I could see them together, in my thoughts. How they're...did you know that they have so much in common that it will be a match made in heaven when they come together?" She told him he'd mentioned that before. "Well, it needs said again. The two of them will be perfect. But her falling over the falls...never saw that one coming. Should have, with her love of children, but didn't see it. I just thought them to be together when she came out to visit with our Addie and all of them. Now this. Not that I would have wished this on anyone, but it's for the best. They'll be fine once they find their ways. I just know it."

"I've looked into Drew's life as you asked me to do. I never knew that he'd been so hurt by her." Grandda nodded, not saying anything. Aster had taken the body of someone to have him look up some information that Grandda had asked her to see too, using the computer that she'd missed out on learning as a teenager. Drew had had a horrific childhood, and there had been no one there to help him as the others had. Even Steele had Ray after she'd died. But Drew had been all alone. "I hate to say this, but it's a good thing she died like she did after what she did to Drew. There's no telling what she might have continued to do after he got out of the hospital that last time."

"Killed him. There was no doubt that was the path that she was on. I never saw him then, but I have seen his memories and his nightmares. The poor boy dreams of her nightly, and none of it is good. Even when he tried so hard to make her love him, she treated him like he was nothing more than a foot fungus. Worse. Something she found under her toenail." Aster thought that was a little gross, but agreed with him. "You go on and see the child's mother. I'll keep an eye on this one for a bit. Cindy might be able to give you some information that you didn't get from the man."

Aster moved to the other end of the hospital to the children's ward. It hurt her to see all the sick and injured babies here. Some were dying from diseases that there was no cure for as yet. Others from accidents, and then there were the ones that their own parents had put there. Beaten with more than just their hands and fists...with items such as chairs and irons, things that no child should ever have used against them. There was even one child that his mother had left in the car all day to die. Had it not been for the quick actions of strangers, he would surely have been another statistic in this cruel and often times horrible world.

And all of these children would wear a mark from these

things. Not all of them seen by others, but felt daily, if not hourly, by the children. Emotional scars—and there were plenty of those for each of them—at times were deeper than any cut that was inflicted, and left bruises worse than any fist could have caused. Parents like some of these children had needed to be treated the same way they had treated their own flesh and blood.

Becky, the little girl, was asleep. Drugs had been given to her so that she could rest easily and heal. Her body, broken beyond what even an adult could stand, was healing, but not quickly, and certainly not without a great deal of pain. The medications that she was given were keeping her still and quiet so that her body would work to make her whole again. Aster saw her mother sitting right next to her child, just as she'd been every time that Aster had come to see the little girl since first becoming aware of her and Mac.

"She's too little for all of this. I'd gladly take her pain if I thought it would help her." Aster moved to stand next to Cindy Rush, Becky's mom. "She shouldn't have been in that water in the first place, much less near those falls by the house. I told him that she was too little for it. But he said she was fine and would have to learn how to manage it. You can see how that worked out. She nearly died, and now she's all alone in this world. For what? Because he wanted things his way, that's all."

"I'm so sorry for you and your little girl, Cindy. But he's worse now than he was before he died. Adam's been bothering the woman that saved your little girl, did you know that?" Cindy said that she hadn't left the child's side, so she had no idea. "She did all she could to save her, and now he wants her to die so that he can get even for his own death."

"He should have died a long time ago. A man like him…I

don't know what I was thinking when I went out with him. And my mother should never have made me marry him after what he did to me. But I got this little ray of brightness in my life because of him. But Adam, I never loved him." Aster knew this. She'd seen the memories of both of them since she'd been coming by to see Mac. "Had she stopped to save us, Becky would have surely died, and that would have killed me anyway. So this is better. What did he think was going to happen to our child should she have done what he said?"

"He doesn't seem to care about anything other than the fact that he's dead. Do you suppose he would have tried to save you as well as his daughter if he'd lived?" Cindy snorted and said not likely. "I don't think so either. He's only out for himself. That woman nearly gave her life to save your daughter. It's not right of him to go in there and try to get her to give up. Can you talk to him?"

"No. I don't…he would rather hit me than to listen. There is no reasoning with him at all when he thinks he's right. Even if the truth of the matter that he's wrong is staring him right in the face. The only reason I stayed with him was because he would have taken Becky from me. I'm not…I had some issues before she was born, and he's held them over me my entire… he's not a good man. And a worse father and husband. There is no talking to him. His word is fact, and there is no changing his mind." Cindy put her finger near her daughter's cheek, but Aster knew she couldn't touch her. "I'd give almost anything to hug her again. Touch her soft skin. Feel her breath on my cheek as she spoke to me. Just to hear her voice, see her smile. He did this to us. Took her from me."

"How?" Aster almost told her that she didn't really want to know, but waited as the woman sobbed great heart wrenching sobs that tore at her as well. "Cindy, whatever you

27

can help me with, I swear to you he'll never know."

"I don't care now. I want...." Cindy looked at her then. "You're his sister, aren't you? That man that I've heard about since...since I died. Steele Bennett. You're his sister, aren't you?"

"I am. And if you want, I can have him come and talk to you." Cindy shook her head and looked at her daughter again. "Cindy, your husband, what did you mean when you said that he did this to you?"

"He told her that she was going to learn to swim or drown. Tossed her into the water without so much as a care as to what I was telling him, or even begging him, to do. When she hit the water further downstream than I thought she should have been, I jumped in after her. I can't swim either, but for her I would have.... I just couldn't get to her. Then that woman, she just went after her like some sort of avenging angel, and I knew, deep in my heart, that she was going to be safe. But Adam, he hit the boat from behind on purpose like he knew that it was going to tip them over the edge. Then he went down too. I was never so happy in my life. But I got caught up in the water and couldn't stop myself from following him."

~~~

Drew watched the puppy...a dog, really. The pure bred German Shepard was all feet and legs, but he was beautiful, and friendly. Drew wasn't sure what to do with him, but he didn't seem to care. Playing fetch was fun for a while, but Drew thought it was pretty boring. But apparently the dog could have done it all damned day. When the soggy mess was dropped at his feet again, Drew looked at the dog.

"You should learn to toss this yourself; you know that, right?" A soft yip was his reply. "Look Rory, why don't you think of something else? I mean, there are about two hundred toys in that box over there. Get something else for me to toss so I can have a little change of pace."

The dog ran off as if he understood every word he'd said to him. As he went through his toy box, bigger than most kids' toy boxes, Drew went to sit on the steps of the deck and watch the water go by them.

Rory had greeted him at the door like they'd been long lost friends. It was nice, Drew thought, to have someone so excited to see him. As they wrestled on the floor for about twenty minutes, Drew realized he was having fun. The dog was too. And after getting him some food and clean water, he'd taken the dog and himself out to the wrap around deck and played there as well. Now he wanted to do something else.

When Rory came back with a leash, Drew wondered what the hell he was supposed to do with that. Walking him for sure, but where? There wasn't a lot of houses around the area…in fact, this one was so far off the beaten path that he'd passed the driveway four times before he finally found it. And what a house it was too. There was a house that was close to the road that he'd seen, but that was about it. But this one had that one beat all to hell and back with its beauty and view.

The log cabin had been modified several times from the original house. He knew this because there were pictures in the living room of the progression of the work done. And it looked as if Mac had done a great deal of it on her own. The small house, probably the living room where the television was, had been there first, and after what appeared to be several facelifts, the house now had a second and third floor, as well as extending well beyond the drive that had been there to include a larger living room and office. A dining room and two bedrooms had been added to the main floor. One was being used as an office, the other was a library that was as well stocked with an assortment of paperbacks as he'd bet most bookstores were. And there was a large working kitchen.

The second and third floor hosted two bedrooms each. Both had their own bathroom, as well as a walkout deck that hung out over the river it was near. Large picture windows graced the front and back of the house, affording a view that was breathtaking no matter the time of day or night. Drew felt at home in the house. Comfortable. More so than he had ever felt in his new house. He supposed it had a lot to do with the décor, too.

The entire place was done up in warm earth colors, from the hardwood floors in the living room to the dark red pillows that were on the deep leather couches. A pretty foot blanket was on the back of both, and one was folded up on the foot stools at the foot of each of the four chairs that were also scattered around the room.

The room he'd taken as his own while there was also warm and friendly. The comforter was dark blue, the shutters — no curtains in any part of the house — were the same deep color and made the room feel like it had been made with him in mind. Earth tones were his favorite colors, he thought suddenly with a smile, and wondered if the woman could come to his house and help him make it look like someone lived there and didn't just hang around, as he had been doing.

Just as he made his way to his room he saw a woman coming up on the front porch. He didn't go to the door when she knocked. Drew knew what Sandy looked like, as she'd met him at the door earlier when he'd come by to see to the dog. She assumed that he would be staying and had filled not just the cabinets with food for him and the dog, but the pantry, as well as the freezer and refrigerator. This woman was not

Sandy. And if the low growl from Rory was any indication, she wasn't over for tea often either.

"Hello?" He said nothing but did put his hand out to Rory when he came to stand beside him. Another low growl from the dog gave him all the help he needed in continuing to ignore the woman and stay where he was. "Hello? I need to talk to whoever is staying here for the dog. You need to know a few things. I know that you're in there, I just saw you playing with the stupid dog."

Drew knelt down to the dog and was rewarded with a wet lick on his face. But when Rory moved closer to him and growled again when the doorknob was turned, Drew felt his body stiffen with fear.

"Damn it all to hell. Come to the door. I know that you're in there." Drew ran his hand down Rory's back to smooth out his fur when it began to stand up. "I want to talk to you about selling this place when the woman who lives here dies. You need to know that she said she'd give me first refusal. I want you to know that I'm going to buy it. You need to come out so I can tell you all about it."

"What do you think, boy? Do you think that your mistress will want her to have it if she should die?" Rory growled. "Yeah, I didn't think so either, and I don't even know her. But that woman at the door, she's not going to go away any time soon, is she?"

Drew went to the door and pulled it open just as the woman put her hand out to knock again. She just stared at him and he at her for several minutes before the woman started to pull open the screen door. Her smile made him think of vultures on the lookout for prey. He pulled the door closed and locked the little hook over the circle and stood there.

"I thought I'd come in and talk to you." Drew said nothing

31

to her. "You're not very friendly, are you? Not that it matters. Neither is the woman that lives here. But here I thought we'd have a nice talk about things."

"No." She nodded, but he could see the smile on her face begin to crack. "My sister has no intentions of selling her house to anyone. And she's not going to die. So I have no idea what you think you're about, but I'll call the police if you try that shit again. Now, tell me what you wanted so I can get back to what I was doing. Playing with the stupid dog, as you called him, is better than talking to a liar."

"Mac doesn't have a brother, so who's the liar now?" Drew crossed his arms over his chest but said nothing. The woman began to look a little flustered now. "I'm pretty sure she might have mentioned you when we spoke about her selling me—"

"She never had a conversation with you about the house, selling it or otherwise. Stop trying to make yourself out to be something you're not to her. The dog hates you, or at least has a beef with you, so Mac wouldn't have had you in her house for all the money in the world." The woman looked back at her car then at him again. "What do you want?"

"I want this house. And everything that goes with it. I have no idea why she even…what does a single woman want with a house this big? She doesn't even entertain. I would. This place would be a showplace when I'm done with it. And let me tell you, I have big plans for this whole area." Drew told her the house was beautiful now. "You have no idea what that even means, I'm betting. If you're really her brother then you know that she won't be able to come here after she gets home, if she even gets to leave the hospital in one piece. Last I heard she was near death twice now, and not going to be right in in the head when she does get out."

Drew looked down at Rory, and then he reached up and

removed the little lock from the screen. Pushing it open just enough for Rory to get out, he wasn't surprised when the woman started to come in. Rory nearly knocked her on her ass in his haste to get out. Drew told the dog to get her off the property, and nearly fell over laughing when the dog did just that. He was still on the porch when the car peeled out of the drive and Rory came back to him with a bit of silk in his mouth.

"Good boy. I'm betting that you've done this before." He petted the dog a bit more before he snapped the leash on his collar and started for the back deck and tree line. They could both use the exercise now that they'd had their fun.

The property was bordered on two sides by the fast moving river. Drew would bet anything that the dock and boats belonged to Mac, as did the large building that housed fishing equipment and a large fridge filled with water bottles. Inner tubes were on the walls, as well as ice skates and hockey equipment. This woman played as hard as she worked, he'd bet.

There were awards in the building too, all naming Mac as the winner. She had participated in a great many sports when she was younger, and had been pretty good at them all. There were also pictures of her father, standing by her side when a much younger Mac was holding up one award or another. Framed certificates called her a humanitarian, as well as a good mentor. In one part of the building were boxes of more awards, all of them stating what a wonderful athlete she was. Some of them were dated as recently as several weeks ago.

Drew moved out of the building when Rory whimpered. He supposed that the dog missed his mistress too.

The chairs on the long dock were all anchored down with a chain, and each of them had been painted recently. He could tell which she favored when she was out here, and sat on the one that looked to be the closet to the water. Drew could see why she loved it here so much. Taking the leash off Rory, he let the dog run up and down the edge of the water, and even threw a ball at the edge for him to retrieve. It was a game that Drew figured he and his mistress had played a great deal. When his alarm sounded, it startled him to realize that it was nearly time for him to go sit with Addie.

At ten minutes before he was to be at the hospital, he was making his way to the room. Addie could only see Mac for ten minutes every hour, and she talked to her every minute she was there. It haunted him to see his friend this way. She was scared for Mac, and to be honest, so was he. In the little time he'd spent at Mac's home, he was beginning to see the woman as she had been.

"Would you mind if I took a little walk? I need to talk to Nick, and I have no service in here." He told Addie that he'd go with her. "No. Please don't. I need a little bit of time to myself. I'm all right. I'm just…it's almost too much. If you'd just stay with her, I'd really…I need just a few minutes."

Drew stood in the visitor's area and waited. He'd forgotten to ask when the next visit was, and was surprised to see Alexandra, Vinnie's grandmother, fade into the room with him when the nurse came to tell him he could see Mac now. Before he could tell her that he'd wait on Addie, Alexandra said they'd be right there.

"She's not going to make it through the night." Drew sat down hard when Alexandra spoke after the nurse left. "I have it on good authority that she will have an aneurysm at around two in the morning, and they won't be able to save her. I want your permission to save her life."

"Mine?" She nodded and sat down before him. "I don't

know why you'd need mine. I don't know the woman at all. Perhaps you need to talk to Addie. They're very close. I'm only here because Nick asked me to keep an eye on his wife."

"No. It's you." He started to tell her no again when she continued. "Addie won't let me. Not because she doesn't love her friend, but she knows for a fact that there is a DNR on her paperwork. She'll follow Mac's wishes because she knows that's what she wanted."

"And you think I won't want to follow those some guidelines for what reason? You do know that it's really bad form of you to tell me and then ask me to go against her wishes, right?" He was almost afraid of the answer. "Please tell me this wasn't a plot to get me a wife. I will never forgive you if it is."

"It's not." He knew that she was keeping something from him, but he looked down the hall at the door where Mac was. She would die, he had no doubt of that. "She's a good woman. And so you know, she's a great deal like you and the rest of the men. Her death, this final one, will cause a ripple through the necromancy world that will be felt for generations. She is needed here and now."

"That doesn't answer my question as to why me." She nodded and stood up. He had no choice but to follow her. As they stood outside the doorway, he thought of all the reasons why he didn't want to make this decision. "What aren't you telling me?"

"She is for you." Drew nodded. He had no idea why, but he had thought that was the reason. It didn't make the decision any less hard, but he knew now that there was a rhyme and reason to this all. "If you let her die, you will be alone for the rest of your life, Drew. You don't want that. To be alone when there can be such joy in your life with her."

35

"I like being alone." Alexandra said nothing. "And if I do this, allow you to do whatever it is that you need to do to save her, what happens if she hates me? Or I her."

"You are nearly in love with her now." Not true, but he said nothing. "You know me well enough to know that what I say to you is true. You must allow me to save her. If not for you, then for Addie. And her child."

He looked at Alexandra, then at the door again. He had a feeling that Addie was going to be hurt by this if Mac didn't make it. He'd never seen her, or anyone for that matter, so broken up by another's pain and suffering. Looking at Alexandra, he nodded once and entered the room. Drew had a feeling he was going to regret this for the rest of his life. If not beyond that.

CHAPTER 3

Mac nearly screamed when she opened her eyes again. She'd done it before, she knew this, but like now, there had been too much pain and she'd gone under again. Right now, while the pain was less, there was so much…so much going on around her that she knew that something was wrong with her. As the room and the things in it began to settle and take shape, she realized that she was hooked up to something that was making her gag. The need to jerk it from her mouth had her reaching for it, whatever it was.

"Don't move." The voice, strong and full of authority, had her pausing. The person, a doctor she thought, moved into her line of vision and she could only make out that he was wearing light clothing and something shiny around his neck. "I'm going to take this out now, so I want you to lie as still as you can. All right?"

Fear and something akin to horror made her stare at him. Her vision was still blurry, but the sights and sounds—the beeping of a machine, a woman crying quietly to her right, and the light shining in her eyes—were making her want to lash out. Instead she lay still, keeping her fear to herself. When she felt whatever it was run up her throat then out of her mouth, Mac felt the tugging of it all the way to her toes.

The man, the doctor, told her to just breathe.

The pain all over her body, was the next thing she felt. Even her hair seemed to be telling her that she was hurt beyond what she'd ever been before. The man stood in her line of vision again, and she could see that he was smiling. Mac wanted to hit him in the mouth.

"You've been in an accident." No shit, she wanted to tell him, but only nodded as best she could. There was something holding her head still, a brace she figured. And no matter what held her, nodding her head had been a mistake. Every part of her head was telling her that she had to not do that again, and even her belly was protesting the movement. "You're in County Hospital and have been for several days now. I've been seeing to your injuries. My name is Doctor Phillip Manchester. Do you remember what happened to you?"

There was a woman there in the room with them. For some reason Mac could make her out a great deal better than she could the doctor. But there was something off about her too, something…she was hurt, and badly.

"Help her." Mac's voice sounded broken even to her. Like a record that had been out in the sun too long and skipped and jumped. Mac loved old records and knew the sound well. When the doctor turned to look where she was, he frowned when he looked back at her. "Help her."

"Who? There is no one there." Mac wanted to point out that she was there and was in need of help when the woman shook her head and smiled. It was…there was too much damage done to her face and neck for her to be anything but hurt. "Miss Mackenzie? What do you see?"

"Don't tell him, Mac. He won't understand and he'll think you're mad. I'll explain when he leaves you. All right? But I have to say, it's nice to see you awake. So many people have been worried for you." Mac thought perhaps she might have hit her head. The woman, a young girl actually, smiled at her again and told her that they'd talk later. "My name is Aster Bennett, by the way. I'm going to explain a great deal to you when we're alone."

Mac said nothing to either of them. The doctor was going on about her injuries, which were making themselves known with each mention of them. And the girl was moving about the room looking at the flowers that Mac had only just noticed, staring out the window as if there were a great show going on, and coming back and forth to her, warning her not to say anything to the doctor. When the doctor left, telling her that he'd be back, Mac tried to think what had happened to her.

"You saved a little girl, do you remember that? She was going over the falls when you snatched her up out of the water." Bits and pieces were coming back to her as Aster spoke. "You did go over, sadly, but you survived and so did little Becky."

The falls. Winding Falls down from her home. She had come upon a family, or at least they looked to be a family, trying to get to a child. The little girl she'd gotten up out of the water, only to take her over the falls with her.

"I thought...I thought we were going to die." Aster nodded as if she knew that had been going through her mind when she'd felt the kayak shift and move over the falls. "Her parents?"

"Both dead, I'm afraid." Mac had figured they might die when she saw them in the water. The current wasn't very choosy about who it pulled under its spell. And none of them had any kind of life jackets on, even though it was posted everywhere that the current was strong there and could be deadly. "Becky's father has been to visit you. Not Cindy as yet. But now that you're awake, she said she'd come by."

"I thought you said...." Mac closed her eyes when she thought that Aster moved through a chair that was near her. Her mind was playing tricks on her or something. "He's dead, you said."

"He is." Mac looked at Aster and closed her eyes again when she smiled. "So am I. I was killed a very long time ago when I was seventeen. You'll be able to see a great many ghosts now that you've been to the other side and back. And you'll be able to do a great...."

"I don't know what you're doing, but I'd like to be left alone now. You have a really sick sense of humor and I don't care for it." Aster didn't move but stood where she was. "Who are you really? And how are you doing this?"

"I'm dead. And so are Adam and Cindy Rush. You saved their daughter when she was nearly ready to go over the falls. By doing what you did when you did, you saved her from being killed when the rocks and water took you both under. Without your help, she would have surely drowned as her mother did." Mac didn't look at the girl as she continued. "I'm sorry that you've been told this way, truly I am. But you have to know so that when he comes here, and he will, you can deal with him. You'll be able to see him, just as you are me. A shadow of himself, a ghost, as I am."

"I don't want to deal with anyone." The pain, soft at first, was making her sick with it. She hurt in more places than she could name; and not only that, she was sure that before this was all over, she was going to be in a great deal more pain. "Just go away and leave me alone."

There wasn't anymore conversation, but Mac wasn't sure that the woman was gone. It made her sick to try and focus on any one thing for very long, so she kept her eyes closed.

Aster, or whoever she was, seemed to be off her rocker, and Mac didn't want any part of it. As Mac tried to think beyond the pain, which was getting worse by the second, she felt tears roll down her cheeks. Opening her eyes when someone said her name, she nearly sobbed when the nurse told her that she was giving her something for her pain. As the meds filled her bloodstream, Mac was sure that she could see more hurt people milling about her room. Closing her eyes again, not just against the pain but everything, she let herself drift away on the magical drug that took the pain away.

When she woke up the next time, Mac felt better. There wasn't anything in her throat this time, and she could move her hands now. When she turned her head to the right, she saw Addie sitting there asleep and a man sitting in the chair looking at her. He stood up and came to her, bringing her a glass of water.

"You have to drink slowly. They said you can have sips, but not much more than that. Okay?" She nodded at him and filled her mouth with the water as soon as the straw touched her tongue. Holding the ice cold liquid in her mouth, she looked up at the man standing over her. "My name is Drew Mullins. I'm a friend of Addie's."

The water felt wonderful as it trickled down her throat. She wasn't going to swallow it, knowing that if she did, she'd hurt again. And more than likely throw up. She'd been hurt before enough to know that sudden cold could react badly with an empty stomach. As soon as it was a manageable amount, she swallowed slowly and felt the coldness of it all the way to her belly. He offered her another drink but she told him no.

Trust. There was something about this man that she trusted. Mac didn't trust easily, nor did she do it upon first meeting someone. But this man, Drew, made her feel that she could not just tell him her deepest darkest thoughts, but she could depend on him as well. For anything.

"I had a strange dream before." Talking was easier now too. As if since whatever had been in her throat had been removed, it had healed over. Frowning, she looked up at Drew as he stood over her. "This young girl came to talk to me. She said she was a ghost…well, she said she was dead. I don't think she really believed she was a ghost."

"That would be Aster. And she does believe it because that is what she is. A ghost, I mean. You'll be seeing a great many of them as time goes on." Mac felt the chill of his words make the water in her belly churn up. "She told me that she spoke to you, and was afraid that she'd upset you."

"I'm not seeing ghosts." Drew said nothing but set the water back on the bedside table. "I can't see ghosts. No one can. I'm not sure what's going on here, but I don't want to hear that again."

"If you say so." He didn't say anything more as he sat back down in the chair. It occurred to her that he was handling her, and she didn't like that. Before she could ask him to leave, he began talking again. "The doctors are very happy with your progress. It was touch and go there for a while. And now that you're on the mend, we should talk about what you're going to do when you're released from here. Oh, I've seen to Rory for you. I hope you don't mind, but Sandy insisted that I stay at your house to care for him. I think we've both been very happy with each other."

"He's my dog." Mac felt stupid as soon as the words were out of her mouth. "I'm sorry. I've been…I don't do well with people. I'm more at home being alone."

"As am I. But back to your dog. I've convinced the staff

here that he's your stress companion and that you would do better with him nearby. I hope you don't mind." He nodded to her left and she turned to that direction. "He's been sleeping there since you were transferred to a regular room. I take him for walks when he wants out, and we both go back to your house when Vinnie comes in to keep an eye on Addie. He's been the model pup and a good all-around friend to me as well."

"No, I don't mind. And thank you for caring for him. He's all I have." She watched her dog as he slept. Rory was a good companion, and she was glad to see him doing so well with this. "He's not given you any trouble, has he? He can be a little on the annoying side when he wants something."

"No. Like I said, he's a good dog and he's well trained. We've played fetch a great deal, he does like that game, and the two of us have taken long walks around your property. Speaking of which, your neighbor, Mrs. Dutch, is a piece of work. She has it in her head that you're going to sell." Mac knew that and turned to look at Drew to agree. But she saw Addie was awake now and nearly burst into tears when she came to her with her arms wide open.

~~~

Addie had never been so glad to see someone in her life as she was Mac. As they cried and held each other as best they could, Addie saw Drew take Rory out of the room and close the door softly behind him. She was worried about Drew if she was truthful with herself, and also about what he was going to do when he left for home tomorrow. His time here was up and he had to go back to work. But Nick was coming out, and for that she was thrilled.

"I've been so afraid for you. I talked to Sandy the day after your accident and she said you'd been hurt. I came as soon as I could to be with you." Mac didn't let go of her hand, but held her as Addie pulled her chair over. "You scared us to death. I've been...don't do that again, all right? I need you to be there for me when I pop this kid."

"I'm sorry. I'll try my best not to do anything to worry you again. But I don't know a great deal about what happened. Just starts and stutters, I guess you could call it. I think...the little girl, Becky I think her name was, she's all right then?" Addie told her that she was still in a medically induced coma, but they expected her to be taken out of that soon. "She's...she was drowning when I saw her. I had to help her. Her parents should have known better than to put someone so little in that river like that. She didn't even have on any kind of life vest, much less a person there to keep her safe."

"Of course you had to help. And I agree with you about her parents. There is more to the story than just what you think, but I'll tell you about it later." Addie watched Mac's face and wondered how much of what happened she remembered. "You're going to be all right now. They said that they think you might be the quickest recovery from near death they've ever seen."

"I actually feel really good. Better than I did earlier when I woke up. I guess they were wrong about how bad it was." Addie could see the doubt on her face, but she didn't say anything. There was time enough for her to explain what had happened. But for now, she was going to enjoy having her back. "That man that was here, he said you and him were friends. Is he really living at my house? And taking care of Rory for me?"

"Yes. I hope it's all right. He's been taking care of it while you were here. Mrs. Dutch is under the impression that you're going to sell the house to her or some other such nonsense, and she's been telling Drew that it was an unwritten agreement between the two of you. He's set her straight, I think."

"She's a bitch." Addie laughed. It was the same thing that Drew had said about her. "When I bought the land and the house, it wasn't much. An old shack that was doing its best to try and fall down around my head. Now that I've got it the way I want it, she's been all over me to sell. Me and a couple of other houses that are around where I live. She's an idiot if she thinks that we're going to roll over for her. I hope she's not given him much in the way of trouble."

Addie assured her that he'd not said so, only to tell her what she'd said to him. They spoke about nothing important really. She'd called her when she'd found out about the baby and Mac was so happy for her, but Addie could tell she was getting tired. As soon as Mac's eyes drifted closed again, this time not opening right away, Addie moved to the window to watch Drew with Rory in the courtyard below her.

"They're perfect together." Addie didn't turn to look at Aster, but watched as Rory brought a ball back to Drew and he threw it again. "I know that you're mad at me still, but we had to do something. He might have left without getting to know her."

"She's not going to be any happier than Drew is when they find out what you did. Both of you, Alexandra and you, lied to him. She was no closer to death than I am." Aster said nothing and Addie turned to look at her. "Why did you do this, really?"

"Adam Rush is going to harm her. You know that as well as we do." Addie said nothing. She'd seen the man a couple of times while she'd been here, but never long enough to take care of him. There were rules even the dead had to abide by, and he was in trouble. "And she is for Drew. We know that

45

for sure now."

"You know that now? And what if she'd not been for him? What if they hated each other on sight? What would you have done then? End one or both of their lives?" Aster looked shocked and Addie felt horrible. "I'm sorry. I know you wouldn't do that. I'm just…she's my best friend and has been for most of my life. I feel like I've done something horrible to her. And to Drew."

"There's more, as you know. His mother is coming for him. And when she does, we're all afraid that if he doesn't have Mac in his life, he will end it. He's that close, Addie. Even you have seen it." Addie looked down at Drew. She knew now what he'd had done to him. Aster had come to her last night and told her everything. Drew had had a worse life than all the others put together, and she had never known. After talking to Nick and Steele, she knew they hadn't either. They had guessed, but never pried into his life when he didn't seem inclined to share. It wasn't the way they did things. Most of the time anyway. "When she finds him again, which she will soon, she will bring him low, to the point where he feels he has no reason to live again. And you know as well as I do that neither Steele nor you can banish her without Drew's permission. No matter what she does to him short of causing his death, she is his to deal with."

"She should have been banished long ago. Long before he even began working for the team." Aster told her that she agreed. "To do the things she did to him. What sort of person does that to their own child? Who treats someone that way for no other reason than they can? And to continue to haunt him, terrorize him like he was nothing more than a stranger she met on the street."

"I don't know. Her mind was gone long before Drew was

born, and then after he came to her, she no longer tried to keep control over her emotions or her sanity. There was no reason for her to try to be sane, to show them she was fit to receive welfare. They gave it to her because she had a child." Addie thought that was the stupidest thing she'd ever heard. It was like she'd heard recently, you had to have a license to drive, but any asshole could destroy a kid.

"You're going to tell him what you've done and why. And her, aren't you? What you've done to save her life? I know that...you know that she's going to not believe you. I overheard her talking to Drew. She does not believe in what we do at all." Addie wasn't worried that she'd have a fit over finding out there really were ghosts and people talked to them. Mac, if nothing else, had a very open mind. "She might want to hurt someone. And right now, I'm hoping it's you or Alexandra."

"Alexandra will tell her when the time is right. Drew too. As more and more of us come to see Mac, she'll learn to see what she can do. And we can talk to her too. Drew will explain what she needs to cope and make it work. He...he knows that Mac is his other half." Addie looked at Aster when she spoke. "He's not happy, in the event you didn't get that. He's terrified of what his mother will do, as you are. I don't think...he's going to have to have Mac at his side or he'll never survive her again. Not now."

"You think she'll kill him. Or make him kill himself. Either way, he'll die when she comes for him." Aster nodded. "I think you're wrong about that. I don't think he'll let her convince him that he needs to end his life. She might hurt him, but he's a great deal stronger than you think he is."

"I hope so. But she won't go that way. She'll drive him mad. Drive him over the edge of reason until he feels that there is no choice but to end his suffering and get her out of his life. She'll do that to him. Not because she wants him there for any nefarious reasons. But with the hold she has over him because, despite it all, he did love her very much." Addie could understand that, she supposed. She and her father hadn't had the best of relationships when she left him, but he was still her father. "Addie, we're going to get them through this. Alexandra only did what she had to do."

"So you said. And now...what will they do when they find out that they're going to live forever? How do you think they're going to take that?" Aster said she didn't know. That Alexandra had done that on her own. "Is that why she's not been around? Because she knows that I'm pissed off?"

"Yes." Aster's grin disarmed some of her anger. "She's still very afraid of you. I think she believes you will do something to her that will make her less than she is. I'm not sure what that would be, but she is avoiding you all the same."

Addie might have thought that was funny if she wasn't so mad at them both. They had conspired against the couple, both of them. That wasn't really what they'd done, but both of them were her friends, and she hated seeing them manipulated like they had been. First with Drew in thinking he had made a life or death decision concerning someone he didn't really know. And with Mac in that her life had been turned upside down, and would continue to be so until this was taken care of. Neither of them had been told the truth since this terrible thing had happened.

Drew entered the room about ten minutes later. The dog, Rory, went to his big bed and laid down, but not before going to his master and putting his head on her hand. He loved her, that much was obvious, and she was pretty sure that Drew loved the dog as well. He certainly seemed to be having a

48

good time with him.

"I have to leave soon." Addie looked at Drew with a heavy heart. "I'm on call and I have to get back to get my gear ready in the event we have to go out. Nick told me that he's traded around with Hugh, and that he's coming out to see you for his week."

"He is. And I wish you could stay. But I know that they need you." Nodding, he looked over at Mac, who was still sleeping. "She's going to be coming home with me if I can convince her to do so. She'll need time to heal where she's not going up and down stairs."

"She'll hate that. I would. Her house is nothing like yours. Pretty, yes, but hers all the same." He would hate that too... depending on others to help him. Addie had never realized how much they were alike until now. "Will you bring Rory with you too? It might make her feel better."

"You too, I'm betting." He only flushed and she smiled at him. "Drew, would you like to take him back with you now? It might give Mac a good reason to not fight me about coming to stay with me."

"I would, but I won't. They need each other." Nodding again, she watched him as he moved closer to the bed. "I've never seen her face. I mean, it's been so swollen and bruised. I'm betting she's a real beauty. Not that it matters, but I bet she's beautiful. There are a few pictures of her with her dad, but nothing of her after about the age of thirteen, I think."

"She is. Her dad was her world, and when he died, she did a little as well, I think. Since we were in college together and even after, she's been a real fitness nut. There were times when I thought for sure she was going to kill herself with one of her stunts. But I guess it's paid off well. She is very successful at what she does, and people enjoy her games, as she calls them." Drew ran his finger down Mac's cheek, then turned to her. "I'm going to miss you."

"And I you." He looked...well, she thought he looked like he needed to say something, but wasn't sure how to go about it. As he stood there, just looking lost, she thought of what had been done to him and wanted to tell him. But he spoke first. "I know."

It took her several seconds to try and work out what he meant. And even after the million things ran through her head that he could know made the circle, she was very cautious about asking him about what.

"That she wasn't dying. I know for a fact that her prognosis was good. Better than it had been, and they expected her to heal; while not whole, she was on the mend." She asked him why he'd agreed then. "I talked to a few of the nurses that are wandering around here. Ghosts, if you will. They were here when Alexandra came to see her before Aster told me she wasn't going to make it. They heard the entire conversation they had about keeping me nearby so I can get to know her. I did it because it was the right thing to do. The right thing to do for her and you."

"But not you." He shook his head. "You're not going to try and make it work for the two of you then, are you?"

"I didn't say that. I'm just not going to...you know, about my mother and the things she's done to me. I wasn't sure at first that you did know, but you've been treating me differently. Acting like you felt sorry for me. I don't want that...I never wanted that from any of you." She nodded, feeling the tears that she'd shed for him come back. "Don't, Addie. I can't stand that, please."

"She hurt you more than...she nearly killed you." He nodded, but said nothing. "How did you find out? Another ghost?"

"Yes. Billy told me. He came to talk to me a few days ago. Told me about the emails going back and forth, the late night calls you've been making to Nick. Who in turn talked to Steele. Had I wanted you to know, I would have told you. Or you could have asked. I might not have told you, but you could have asked." Addie told him that she agreed. "It's too late now, isn't it? But I'm going back now. And I'm going to go about my life, my own life, as if none of this ever happened. What I did, what I agreed to, was for you. Nothing else."

"I'm sorry, Drew. I never meant for this to happen." He told her that he was fine with how it turned out, but not to bother him about it again. "I won't. And I'll talk to the others too."

"Thank you, Addie."

He looked at Mac again and then turned and left. It felt like he was leaving more than just this room, but her life as well. The sorrow of it hurt her badly, and she cried at the thought of losing his friendship.

CHAPTER 4

He was avoiding them. Hugh could see it, even thought it was funny most of the time, but now the man was hurting, and as much as he wanted to give him his privacy, Hugh knew that Drew needed someone. Moving across the lawn of the house they were working at, he cleared his throat before he said anything. That was another thing he'd noticed about Drew, he was as skittish as a cat with a long tail in a room full of rocking chairs. Smiling, Hugh thought he should stop hanging out with the older ghost so much. His sayings were bordering on being as bad as Carlton's. Old and odd.

"Drew?" He looked at him with glazed eyes, and Hugh felt his concern double. "What's going on? I mean, other than this fucking job today. Did you hear from Addie? Did the girl take a turn?"

They had been called out yesterday, just after Drew had come back from where Addie and her friend were. The clients in this case were ready to move on, but there were things they wanted in return for leaving the big hotel. Most of them were small, minor things. Like a little information on a family member. Or one had even asked them to check on the stock he'd purchased several decades ago. It had been hard to explain to him that the company, one that produced and

53

sold slippers, had been bought up by a bigger firm, and the slippers were not being made in the States any longer. The man had been devastated.

"Did you know that people you love can hurt you even from the ground?" He knew this, and was pretty sure that Drew wasn't really asking him a question, but merely stating a fact. "She's here. I think she's found out where I am, and she's coming for me again."

"Your mother?" Drew nodded and looked out over the people lined up in front of the table that Ray and Mitch were manning. Writing down the requests and doing them was working out well. Tiring mostly, but working for the most part. "Is she around now? I mean, is she here now?"

"She's calling to me. Trying to find out where I am so she can come with me all the time. I don't want that."

Hugh didn't think he would either. She was a piece of work, Belinda Mullins was. And she was as nutty as a bag of nuts at Christmas time that had been soaked in vodka and set out too long.

Unlike the rest of the team, Hugh knew exactly what had happened to Drew. Had even seen where she'd set fire to him when he'd been ten. And he was pretty sure that he was the only one that Drew had ever talked to about her. At least until recently, when he'd been found out by Vinnie. He was glad that no one had asked him if he'd had any knowledge about it. He would have given them all an earful about prying.

He and Drew had been drunk one night, sitting around in the smallish house that Drew lived in and eating pizza. A rare treat for them both, as they had been living paycheck to paycheck long before they'd met and started working for Steele. It was that night that Hugh confessed why he had an aversion to men in suits, and Drew told him about his mom.

"Have you made any kind of contact with her? I mean, since you left your house?" Drew told him that he'd not. "Good. You don't want to give her any indication that you're wanting her back into your life. Have you talked to Steele or the others yet?"

He really hadn't expected him to, and wasn't surprised when he said that he'd not. "They know that I'm...I have some things to work out yet. And since they investigated me and found out everything, I'm not sure what I can say to them now. But none of them have asked me about it, for which I'm very grateful."

"You know as well as I do that they can't know it all. There are...you and I both know there is more to the stories than just what they can read about. Your mother had been abusing you for years before the fire. She should have been shot, not killed by accident when her gown caught fire when she tried to burn you alive." Drew winced but didn't back away from him. They knew too much about each other to not be brutally honest now. "Go to Steele and tell him to keep her from coming to see you. That way she'll still be around, not that I'd want that either, but you won't have her sent over to some place that makes her life a living hell, much like she did yours."

"She's my mother." Hugh knew that more than anything was the main reason she was still around. He had had to take some pretty big steps to get rid of his own demons, all with the help of Drew, so he would help him with this. "Ray is motioning for us to come back."

Hugh didn't want to work, he wanted to help Drew. No, it wasn't just that though, he didn't want to work period. Not that he was lazy, but he was sick of working like he was. The week off and two on was better, but he was as close to being burned out as anyone could get. Hugh wanted to end it all. Not just his life, though that would have been good as far as he was concerned, but getting out of this business altogether.

As they made their way back to the table to help out, he thought of the things he wanted to do. Things that had nothing to do with the dead or helping them. Hugh wanted to write. He had been actually, and thought it was enjoyable. Laughing slightly at his first attempt, he was glad now that he'd sent it off with a pen name. He'd never live it down if the rest of them found out. Writing romance novels was a great deal more fun and therapeutic then he'd ever dreamed it would be.

"This man wants someone to explain to him what a credit card is." Hugh cocked a brow at Ray when he laughed a little. "He didn't have them when he was alive, and he's been seeing them when he wanders around and was curious how they worked. And this man needs someone to go to his daughter and tell her that she needs to find his insurance policy and use it for her kids."

"Is there one?" Ray told Drew that he didn't know. "Okay. I'll take the credit card, you can have the policy."

"Gee thanks." As he walked to his car with the man in tow, Hugh asked the man a few questions about the policy. He paused before entering his car, knowing this was going to end badly. "You say that your daughter is not getting your grandchildren what they need, yet she is in the system? What sort of assistance does she get from the government? Housing? Insurance?"

"She gets that card that feeds them. But most of the time she just uses it to buy stuff and sell it to the neighbors so she can have the cash. Can't see what she does with it, but her kids are lacking from it." Hugh got into the car and the man stood next to him. "You can go to her now? Talk to her about the insurance policy?"

"I can, but I'm going to need for you to tell me where it is and who it's with. Was your daughter the one that was named as benefactor on it?" He said that she'd been his only living relative when he passed. "Did you make her the benefactor? Some companies don't assume that's who you want to leave the money for."

"No. But that company that I worked with, they took one out on me and she needs to get that money. It was about twenty grand. That'll go a long way to getting her up on her feet, don't you think?" Hugh closed his eyes and tried to think how to tell this man that the company that took the policy out on him was more than likely the only one that had benefited. "I even know where the paperwork is. Or I did know. She took my old desk with her when they moved her to that housing place she's in. Not fit for humans, I'll tell you that."

"Let me look into this for you first. I want to have all the information I can find before I go there telling her about the money, all right?" The man agreed and smiled at him. "I'm not sure that the news will be good, but I'll look into it. There have been a lot of changes recently, but you might not be a part of it. All right?"

"You do that. Yes sir, you do that. She'll be sitting fine when she finds out about it too." Hugh had a feeling that she'd never know about what her father had assumed for her. "When are you going to start? Soon, I hope."

"Right now." Pulling up his computer, he did a search on the company the man said he'd worked for. Hugh was thrilled to know it was still in business and doing well. He had a feeling it was because they were scamming people with insurance policies rather than doing well from sales, which had tanked for the most part in the last few years. But he also knew that he wasn't the best person in the world to be making judgments on big corporations. Not even on his best day.

Four hours later he had his answer. Not a good one either. After telling the man what he knew and what had happened to the policy, he felt bad enough that he wanted to withdraw money from his own account and help the man out. Then he began looking into the daughter.

"She's taking the money that she makes off of buying groceries for the people around her to her husband in prison." The man, Ken, said that couldn't be right. "She goes to visit him weekly and takes him the cash. He uses it to buy drugs. Not just for him, but for his crew as well. He's not a good person, and as much as I hate to say this, neither is your daughter."

"But my grandchildren, what's to become of them now? They have...just last night they went to bed hungry, and there wasn't a thing in the house for them to even do their homework on. I thought she was struggling because of the way the system was treating her." Hugh asked him why he thought that. "It's all she talks about when I see her. How the housing is too small for her and the kids. How it costs so much to send the kids to school nowadays, with fees and all. She doesn't even have a decent car to take them to school in, and they have to walk when the buses are too early."

"I'm sorry, Ken, but what she's saying just isn't true. Her housing is free. She pays very little for her utilities as well. At least those that are included in the package she gets, which the government provides for her. She gets a little over twelve hundred dollars for food each month, as well as the meals that the kids get at school. Those aren't costing her either, nor are the books that children have to have to go there. The district

58

supplies both breakfast and lunch for them. Fees? As far as my friend, Constance, was able to find out for me, they aren't even paying for their own school supplies."

Ken started shaking his head, but Hugh could see that he was beginning to see his daughter for what she was, and not the picture he'd painted in his head about her. Ken faded in and out, his anger, or something akin to it, making him use up a little more energy than he should have. As he stood there, looking out over the field beside them, Hugh waited for him to tell him what he wanted to do. He knew what he'd do, and might yet call child services on her, but for now, he was working for this man. A man that he'd come to admire for what he had wanted to do for his grandchildren.

"There was this man I knew long ago. He works for the county and tried his best to get people abusing the welfare system to be held responsible for what they were doing to the system he loved. He wanted someone to take better control of people like my daughter. He was a good man, and a better father than I ever was." Hugh told him it wasn't him. "You're kind for saying so, but I didn't make her get her act together enough, and now she's got herself four kids all by different daddies, and she's not even taking care of them. I should have done better by them. Not her, but those kids. I need for you to call him. Tell him what you found out."

"The kids will be in the system them. And as much as I hate to say this, they might not be any better off than they are now." Ken nodded and told him to do it anyway. "All right. I'll do it now."

After explaining who he was and what he wanted, the man, David Newry, didn't speak for several seconds. Hugh thought for sure that he was going to tell him to mind his own business, but he only laughed a little before he spoke again.

"You know old Ken, the girl's father, don't you?" Hugh told him that he'd spoken to him. "Yeah, I just bet you have. He's been...well, let's just say that Ken and I go way back, and the next time you see him, tell him it's about time he saw her for what she is. She's been on my list for a while now, but in deference to that old man, I let her go. Too long, now that I know the whole of it. And I know who you are as well. Or at least the group you work for."

Ken stood there, just looking at the field again, when Hugh told him what was going to happen. His daughter was going to jail, and for a long time too. Just the fact that she was smuggling drug money into a prison was enough to get her kicked up into the bigger boys' park. The kids, David told them, would be kept on his radar, and he'd make sure they got what they needed. It was the best promise the man could give him. Nodding, Ken told him he was ready to go and left him standing there feeling like he'd just hurt a man beyond belief. Hugh really hated his job and life at that moment.

~~~

Mac tried her best not to be pissy. It was difficult enough to try and relax around the people in and out of her house, but the way they were acting around her made her want to hit them all. She looked over at Rory, who had been acting out of sorts for two days now, and patted the bed beside her, then he came to her and laid down on the new bed.

"What if I asked you to go around and bite them all for me to get rid of them? Would that make you feel better?" He whimpered at her and she wondered if he understood her even just a little. "These people are invading our space, big boy; is that what it is? Or do you miss Drew?"

At the sound of his name, Rory perked up. He looked around as if he expected the man to come out of hiding for him. She did as well. There was no earthly reason for her to miss the big man, but she did. And even if they'd only had a handful of conversations, most of which had been over the phone, she missed him. And so did her dog. Mac looked at Addie when she came into the room.

"How many do you see now? More than before, I'm betting." Mac said nothing. She wasn't going to talk about the figures she could see now, and refused to listen to anyone who tried to tell her that it was normal. "Mac, they're not going to go away. They're here to see if you can help them. Like we do."

"I have no idea what you're talking about." Rory whimpered again and she put her hand on his head to scratch behind his ear. "You said that I could stay with you for a little while. If I go there, and I'm not saying I will, are you going to bring up the supposed ghosts again? Like daily?"

"No. I'm pretty sure that sooner or later one of them is going to make you see reason. I wish you would come stay with us until you're better. I need to leave soon, and I will worry all the time about you being here alone." Mac had a feeling she was never going to be alone again, but said nothing. "Please?"

"All right, but only until I get my leg working better." She still couldn't believe how much it hurt to walk. The doctor had shown her the x-rays that had been taken when she'd been brought in, and as far as she could see, there was no way she should walk again, ever. But here she was up and around with a cane or a walker, neither of which she used all that well.

She was exhausted most of the time too, and knew that there was no way she could live in this house by herself. Everything was geared for someone who could get around on their own two feet. And the things she thought that she could take care of on her own were now impossible without help. Bathing being one of them.

"I'll have the plane ready in an hour." Before she could tell Addie that was too soon, she was gone.

Mac looked around the room and the dozen or so people that were there. It had been her plan to ignore them until they left. That hadn't worked so far, and even those that had faded out of the room at some point were replaced with others who would come by to try and get her to talk to them. Most, if not all of them, seemed to know that she was here with Addie, and they wanted Addie to help them too. But it was the name Steele Bennett that all of them knew well.

"He's a good man. Fair too. Not like some of those others around calling themselves helpers of our kind. You'd think they were going to get paid or something, the way they come in and tell our families that they see us. Do you suppose they charge them for that bullshit?" One man had gone on to tell her all the things that Steele had done for the dead. "He's even gotten some justice for us too. That's what we all call him and those that work for him, Justice Men. Never met him in real life, but I'm telling you now, he's our only friend."

Mac had wanted to ask him what sort of justice, but she'd asked for her computer and had looked him up. There were a great many stories about the man and his Justice Men. But she was most intrigued by the fact that Drew worked for him as well. She even cried a little when she read about the day that Aster, Steele's sister, had been killed. The poor man had had a bad hand dealt to him; his mother had been arrested for covering up the fact that Steele's father had killed several people, and his sister was killed the same day.

Less than two hours later she was in a big bed on a plane.

Mac was hurting now, so much so that she'd asked for her pain pills, and didn't skimp on a half dose like she had been doing since coming home from the hospital. Her feeling was that if she was out when they landed, she wouldn't know if they dropped her getting her off the big plane. Closing her eyes, she waited for the drugs to kick in and thought of her life now.

The doctor had cautioned her about trying to do too much too soon. She had had enough experience with sports injuries to know that if the doc said rest was needed, she did it. This to her was no different. She didn't have a medical degree, and while she knew her body better than anyone, she wasn't stupid either. However, the limitations that he'd put on her, even after she was healed, scared her more than anything.

"Are you running away? Won't do you any good, so you know. I'm gonna get you dead, and when I do, you're going to regret every day of your afterlife with me." The voice, so close to her ear, nearly made her scream. But instead of opening her eyes, Mac closed them tighter in hopes that the man would just leave her alone. "Listen to me, bitch. I know you can hear me. Why don't you join me here on this side? You owe me, and I want you where I can make you pay. You had the chance to save me but you didn't, and as far as I'm concerned, you signed your own death warrant when you did that."

Adam Rush had indeed come to see her. A great deal. And when he wasn't tormenting her about what he was going to do to her, he was keeping her awake at night with horrific memories of that day. Mac had even asked to see the video that her cam had taken, and wasn't happy when they told her that it was logged into evidence for now. But she was pretty sure that Adam had watched it. Somehow he'd seen what only a few had.

"You killed me because of your arrogance, and for what? So that brat could live? I'm worth more than ten of her. Did you ever stop to think that I had a lot more to live for than a kid? I could have replaced that kid if I wanted to after she died, but now you took that all from me when you just floated on by me like you had not a care in the world. Christ, I didn't want the thing in the first place, and now it's going to live longer than me. You selfish bitch, you should have died instead of me."

It was on the tip of her tongue to tell him to fuck off, but she held her tongue, knowing somehow that to talk to him would give him power. When he didn't say anything for several seconds, Mac opened her eyes to find two people with her, neither of which looked like they were breathing…and hadn't been for some time. One was old, the other looked like he wasn't much older than her car, maybe fifteen or less.

"My name is Carlton. This young man is Donny. We know that you've not been speaking to us and that's fine for now, but we're here on a mission." The younger man, a kid really, grinned at her. "Steele sent us to keep an eye on you. Did you know that little Miss Becky is going to come with us too when she's released? To Miss Addie's house? And that Cindy is coming along to make sure things are all right with her child?"

Cindy? It took Mac a minute to remember that Becky was the name of the little girl that had been in the water, and Cindy had been her mother. She'd been to see her too, and she'd thanked her, several times, for saving her baby. Mac looked at Rory when he wagged his tail.

"He knows us. Well, not us, but what we are to you. Protectors. Men in white armor to keep the damsel safe." Mac tried to stop the grin, but Carlton saw it. "Oh my, Drew was correct. You are a vison. He said that while he'd never

64

seen you without your injuries, he knew you to be a lovely woman."

"My dog misses him." Mac hadn't meant to speak to him, but there was something so incredibly charming about him that she found herself wanting to talk to him. "You said that Steele sent you? Who is he and why does he care that I'm safe?"

"Adam Rush. He's not going to stop. And since he's keeping himself well under the radar when it comes to finding him, Steele is hoping that he'll be able to take care of him when he comes to visit you. Steele and his men, they're the best at what they do." He came toward her, but Donny, the younger man, just stared at her. Carlton glanced at him, then smiled at her before he spoke again. "He's a little in awe of you. I think he's been reading your walls. At his age, things like you did and do are something of an oddity to him. Me too, if you want to know the truth of it."

She had to think what he meant. "Oh, the pictures. They were hung there by Sandy, my assistant. She said that more people would want to come in and try that crap if they could see someone doing it. I think most people think that they're fake."

"Oh no. Not us. We love...well, I've not seen you at work or play, but some of the others have. There are two of my kind living near you that just about had young Donny and me jealous the way they told the story." Mac felt the drugs pulling at her. Carlton must have seen something, because he stood up and told her to rest. "We'll talk more now that you've acknowledged us. If you'd like, Donny and I would feel honored if you'd let us be your guards while you mend. We won't even tell the others that you've spoken."

"I don't want to see ghosts. They're not real."

Carlton laughed a little and told her it was much too late for that, but she was nearly under by then, the drugs had taken her away.

CHAPTER 5

Drew wasn't happy with the situation. There were things he had to do. Not really much, but to be stuck watching over Mac while she slept wasn't high on his list of things he wanted to be doing. But he had promised Addie that he'd help her out while she was at the doctor. It had been his thought that he was driving her, not babysitting. But when he walked into the room and Mac was sitting in a chair, he nearly left again.

"I was told that you don't want to be here. And if it wasn't for the fact that Rory needs to go out, I'd tell you to go away too. But he needs to get out of this house as much as I do." The dog in question was looking at him like he wanted to cut free of some invisible chain and run at him. Going down on one knee, he snapped his fingers and Rory came at him. "You taught him that, didn't you?"

"Yes. He would run at me when I would come to your house and nearly knock me over. It was either teach him to wait until I was ready for him or wear most of my dinner." He played with the dog for several minutes before he stood and addressed Mac. "And I have no idea what you heard about me coming to sit with you, but I was told you were sleeping a great deal of the time and I didn't want to watch you rest. Talking to you is much better, I suppose."

"You suppose?" He nodded, not letting the smile at her tone get him into more trouble with her than he thought he might already be. "You thought that talking to me was going to be a hardship? Well, why don't you take yourself out of here and leave me to my own boringness?"

"You're not very nice to someone you need, are you?"

He snapped the leash on Rory and took him to the door that led out onto the deck. After telling him to stay, he moved back into the room and picked Mac up. Having her arms wrapped around him was wonderful, but he didn't want to get used to that.

"What the hell are you doing? Put me down, you idiot. Do you want to break your fucking back?" He sat her in the lounger on the deck and handed her a soft blanket that he'd brought out before going to get her. "Why did you do this? Not that I'm complaining...okay, I am, but why would you possibly hurt yourself to bring my nasty self out here?"

"Because you look like you needed to get out as much as Rory did." He handed her the bucket of balls he'd bought earlier. "I was going to play with him, but he might enjoy you tossing them to him better."

She threw two balls before she laid back on the chair. It had cost her, he could see that, but she was getting stronger every day, Addie had told him. As he worked through the bucket with Rory running back and forth in the yard, he kept an eye on her too. When she sat up suddenly he tensed, but relaxed again when he saw who was there.

Carlton looked disappointed to find him there. He would bet anything that he and Mac had been talking for some time now. Neither of them said anything, but he waited for the elderly gentleman to talk to him before he looked in his direction again.

"I've been watching out for that man. He's been around, but young Donny and I, we've kept him at bay. He's getting stronger, so you know." Drew asked him where he was now. "Out with his missus. He isn't any better with her as a ghost than he was as a man. Not much of a man either, if you ask me. I think someone needs to show him that treating a lady like he does is just not done."

Mac said nothing, but that was all right with him for now. "His little girl is doing much better now. They've moved her to a ward with children of her own age. I don't think she understands that she's alone in this world."

"She's not alone." They both looked at Mac when she spoke. "I'm going to see about taking care of her. I know that I can't do much now, but I've been thinking about it and.... Well, I've decided to adopt her, when the time is right."

"She'll be a good addition to your home."

Mac nodded at Carlton, then looked at Drew. He realized that she was waiting for him to say something about it, and he thought she was ready to blast him if he told her that was a terrible idea. But he didn't think it was. In fact, he thought that they both could benefit from being a family.

"You have a nice house for a child. She should learn to swim, however. The correct way, that is." Mac nodded and glanced at Carlton, who was nodding as well. "Also, you should know that I've done some checking, and she's going to need some special care too. Not forever, but enough that she can walk without assistance. The doctors are concerned that she might have some muscle tightening in the mornings when she wakes."

"You don't think I'm dumb for taking on a child I don't know? One that might have nightmares for a while?" He asked her why she thought he'd say that. "I don't know. My attorney said that I'm insane for doing it. But he came around after I explained to him who pays him. Roger is a good guy, if not a little conservative in things like this. He believes that I'd be better off just setting up a fund for her and not taking her on. I disagreed."

"He said that to you?" Mac nodded at him. "I see. And his name, what is it? I think he needs a visit or two from me. Just to set the record straight on a few things."

"It's not important. Carlton said he'd take care of it." Drew looked at Carlton and had to smile. Whatever he'd done to the man, or he'd had others to do him, it must have been epic. Carlton left shortly after that, saying that he'd get right onto things. Drew looked at Mac when she spoke again. "She's going to need someone to love her. I've...her mom comes to see me now and again. We've talked about her needs and how much she will enjoy having me in her life. I think I will as well."

"She told me that...Cindy wants to move on, but she's afraid to leave her daughter alone with her husband out there. I know that he's coming to you; Carlton keeps me informed of it, as well as the rest of us. He's worried for you." Mac nodded and put her hand on Rory when he was close enough. "She never meant for this to happen to her daughter, did you know that?"

"Yes. She told me that too. I...I don't think he cared what happened to either of them." Drew told her what he knew. "So he just dumped that little girl in the water to let her drown. He never even...what the fuck was he thinking? Or was he?"

"I would say that he never thinks his actions are wrong and that his word is law." Drew watched her face. She was angry, that much was apparent, but how she was handling it was what made him smile. "You're very beautiful, aren't you? Especially when your dander is up, as Carlton is fond of saying. Or you have your blush on. I have no idea what that means, but he does have the most colorful sayings at times."

"You shouldn't be saying things like that to me. Not now anyway." He asked her why not. "Well, for one thing, I've not been able to have a good shower in a month. My hair looks like a rat has taken up residency there. My body hurts. Not so much from my injuries, but from inactivity, and I feel like I've been out of touch with the world for too long."

"You're beautiful regardless." He stood up then and decided that he was going to help her. "I'm going to help you up. I know you can't walk far, but you can get down and in the yard for a few minutes. While there, we'll talk about this rat that you have living in your hair, and see what I can tell you about the world since you've been hurt. Not much going on that gives us much of a good feeling, but it's all we have for now."

As soon as she stood up, she stumbled slightly into his arms. Drew held her, not too tightly, but enough to have her body pressed against his in the most delicious way. When she looked up at him, all he could think about was kissing her. Taking her mouth with his. Drew watched her tongue as it slid along her lips, and he wanted desperately to follow it with his own.

"Can I kiss you, Mac?" Her short nod had him leaning down more, holding her upright when her body began to sway toward him. "Christ, the things that are running through my mind right now. Most of which would be nearly impossible with the way you're all hurt. But later, I promise you, we'll work through my list if you want."

"Kiss me, Drew. Please?"

He took her mouth. The kiss wasn't the one that he wanted

to give her. As soon as their lips touched, he wanted it all. Instead, he tasted her. Gently, with just a little of the hunger that he had for her. When he lifted his head to see if she was all right with him, she pulled his mouth to hers again and took him.

Her own hunger fueled his, and before he could think that he might want to slow it down, slow her down, he had her lifted up from the deck and wrapped around him. Holding her legs around his hips, Drew sat down on the bench that was near him and held her to him by cupping her ass and rocking her over him. Never letting go of her mouth, he knew that he had to have her, and made his way down her throat to her shoulder. Lifting her blouse up, tugging her bra out of his way, Drew leaned her back enough to suckle at her nipple.

"More. Please, give me more." Christ, he'd give her all of it if he could, and stood up again to take her to the bed in her room. Laying her out on it, he stood over her and looked down at her bare breasts and how he'd left his mark on her. Dropping to his knees, he pulled the soft pants off her, along with her panties. She was panting as hard as he was when he had her pussy exposed for him. "Please. I need you."

"I need you too, but I want to eat you first."

Her nod was his undoing, and he leaned in and took her heat into his mouth, sucking hard on the swollen clit even as she rode his mouth. The scream of her release had him sliding his fingers into her even as she cried out again that she was coming.

His mouth was flooded with her juices. She was hot, wet, and delicious. Need made his balls fill; his cock, already thick from her being on his lap earlier, needed relief, needed freed from his pants. Using his free hand, he unsnapped his pants and freed his cock. The cool breeze had him moaning against her body.

He knew that he had to be gentle with her. But Christ, the thought of plowing her, taking her to the floor and fucking her until neither of them could move, made him nip none too gently on her clit again and again. When she jerked his head up from her, he could see her need. She wore it like his felt, all over his body inside and out.

"Fuck me." He shook his head. "Please, for the love of all of it, fuck me. I need to feel you inside of me now. Because if you leave me hanging, pain or not, I'm going to hunt you down and beat you to death."

"I don't want to hurt you. And you know that I will if I take you right now." Her hips came up off the bed and he moved his fingers in and out of her faster. "I love watching you come. Come for me, Mac, come for me and I'll come all over your sweet body."

She came, screaming out his name. Drinking from her again, sliding his fingers in and out of her, he fisted his cock painfully. But it wasn't enough. Not nearly enough.

Standing up, his cock in his hand, he fisted himself as he watched her fingers take the place of his. As soon as she came, her body bowing up off the bed, he released on her, his cum spraying her in an arc so high that it hit her mouth and breasts. When she licked his cum off her lips, he came a second time, crying out hoarsely as he felt his balls fill yet again. He wanted to fuck her, and her begging wasn't helping him say no any longer.

He leaned over her now. Drew held his cock at her entrance as he watched her face. The moment he saw pain he was going to stop, even if it killed him. Entering her slowly, filling her body with his own, Drew knew that he was going to come as soon as she tightened around him. And when her legs wrapped around his waist, her pussy taking him deeper than he'd ever been in a woman before, he kissed her, tasting his own release on her mouth even as she came screaming. Drew joined her then, pounding her hard as he emptied himself deep within her womb.

Christ, he thought again, she was beautiful. And he was pretty sure that he was never going to be able to leave her again.

~~~

Mac woke to a darkened room. There was a small bit of light coming from the door that led out to the deck, but for the most part, she couldn't make out where she was. As she started to sit up and get her bearings, the man beside her stirred. Drew. She was in bed with Drew. She was in bed with a stranger.

Not really, her mind tried to tell her. As she moved away from him, trying her best to put distance between them so she could think, Mac moaned softly when he pulled her back into his body. Then when he curled around her, shaping his body to fit hers, she wrapped her fingers into his hand and thought that if she died right now, this would be a wonderful way to go.

He was warm and hard, his body naked from when they'd had sex earlier. Hers was too, she realized. And at some point he'd put a blanket over the two of them. As she laid there, she realized something else. She didn't mind so much being here with him.

As he started to moan in his sleep, it occurred to her that he was having a bad dream. Just before she touched him to wake him from it, she heard him talking. His mother. He was dreaming about his mom.

"Don't, please." Mac hadn't known her own mother. Her

father had raised her alone until his death when she'd turned twenty. But she didn't think that someone should be this terrified when their mother was in their dreams. At least not like he was. And his fear of whatever she was doing to him was making her afraid for him as well. "Please don't hurt me again. I beg of you."

"Andrew?" The voice was distant, but Mac knew that if he continued to call out to her, dream about the woman, that she'd come to him. And Mac had no doubt that it was his mother. "Andrew, where are you? You left me there."

"Drew?" Mac gripped her hand tightly on his arm. The woman, the ghost, was there now, just a shadow of her, but she was getting stronger the longer he was dreaming about her. Shaking him harder had him sitting up straight in the bed, but Mac had a feeling that he was still in the grips of his dream. When he screamed, a blood curling sound that had her covering her ears, she knew he needed her. Shaking him harder, causing her a pain she knew she'd regret later, she lashed out at the woman that was coming in the room with them. "What are you doing? You're scaring the shit out of him. Can't you see that? Get out of here now. You're not welcome here."

"I'm not going anywhere without him. But you will be. What do you mean to be here with my son? Get out, you whore." Unmindful of her nudity, Mac stood up and was proud when she only staggered slightly. "You hussy. You raped my son? Do you think you can get him to come to you by giving him a little pussy? Christ, woman, you'd be better off with me. He doesn't have a shit unless I tell him he does."

"Get out of here before I get really pissy with you. And if you call me a whore again, bitch, all bets are off." When the woman came at her, her body — or whatever it was they had —

slammed into her own, and Mac felt her belly lurch. When she started to fall forward, Mac cried out when she was lifted up into strong arms. Drew. He had her. Sobbing hard, she held him to her as she was carried to the bed and put there.

He didn't hold her like she wanted, but got dressed. It hurt, but she didn't comment. When her crying seemed to be finished, she looked at him. Pulling the blanket up over her body, she waited for him to say something, anything, to explain what had just happened.

"I'm sorry." Well that wasn't a good start, her heart thought. "I shouldn't have touched you. Not knowing that she'd come here sooner or later and find me. It was wrong of me, no matter what I thought about...I should never have done this to you."

"Sorry for what, Drew? That your mother came here and called me a whore, or that you had sex with me? I'm really curious which one you're sorry for." He got up to pace and she pulled the blanket tighter around her. The sudden chill in the room had her thinking that she'd never be warm again. "Answer me, damn it."

"Both," he snapped at her. "She's been trying to find me since I left her two months ago. Right before I went to help Addie out. She's not.... I don't want to have anything to do with her anymore. But she doesn't seem to get it. My mother haunts me, and there isn't anything I can do about it."

Mac just stared at him. This was a man who, from all accounts, dealt well with the dead. He was helpful, courteous, and seemingly loved what he did. Now he was telling her that he had no idea how to deal with his own mother? He was either dense as hell or he wanted to hurt her.

"Get out of here." He turned mid pace and looked at her. "You heard me, I want you to go away and not come back."

76

"I want to explain it to you." She waited for ten seconds, then got up. It wasn't easy for her, but she managed to get up without his help, even slapping his hands away from her when he tried to help her pull on her clothing from earlier. "Stop being stubborn and let me help you."

"Get away from me." He backed up when she used her voice, the one that Sandy told her made grown men whimper when they tried to tell her she was wrong about something. "I don't want your help. You need to...you need to grow some balls and deal with her. Does it even bother you that she called me a whore?"

"Yes. I'll deal with her on that. I didn't know she would do that." She studied him. Really looked at him. "What is it? I said I'd tell her not to call you that again. What else did she say to you?"

"You're afraid of her. You...the scars on your back; she did that, didn't she?" He took a step back from her and she knew. "You tell me what happened, or so help me I'll call her back and ask her myself."

His anger took him. It wasn't something that she might have believed if someone had told her that Drew could get angry so quickly. The power of it seemed to drench him. She did that, let her anger take her only to have it run its course quickly and leave like it had come. But she had a feeling that Drew had been storing his up for a very long time. And she was going to feel it.

"You want to know? Fine. I'll tell you. I was ten years old and she tied me to the canopy of her bed. It really wasn't a canopy so much as some PVC pipe taped to her bed so that she could hang me from it when she wanted to beat me. I knew all too well the feel of a belt on my back. A few times, when she could find it, there was this whip. Over and over she'd beat me with it until I passed out or she grew tired. Most of the time it was me passing out that made her stop. But bright and early the next morning she'd start again. Until she was satisfied that I had learned my lesson." She asked him what she thought he'd done. "Nothing. It was never anything that she could pinpoint, other than the fact that she hated me. Oh yeah, I heard that hourly. She told me countless times how much she wished she'd smothered me in my crib. Dropped me into a dumpster if she could have. And if she could have afforded it, she'd have someone kill me for her. Have a stranger hit me with their car. Hell, she didn't care if they raped me so long as I was gone and she didn't have me around anymore. But the thought of losing her food card, that scared her more than anything."

"Don't." She didn't want to hear any more, but he didn't seem to hear her. He pulled his shirt up and over his head. The buttons that were in his way pinged off the walls and floor as he continued.

"Then one night she said enough was enough. It was my birthday…I'd turned ten. But who knew that it would be the one that I remembered for the rest of my life, and not for any good reason other than she died that day. I'd done all I could for her, and all I asked her for was some pizza. Hot and delivered to me like a real person, not having her fuck the man out of it or from a dumpster. I heard later that she'd lost some of her check, as she called it. If there ever was any money coming in, I never saw it. So she tied me to the bed, and hung me there while she beat me." Shaking her head, she looked at his back when he turned. "Then she went to find the lighter fluid. I woke with it being sprayed all over my back, her laughing insanely as it hit my legs and arms. Then I heard it. The sound no person would ever mistake for anything but a match being lit."

"Stop. Please. Just stop." Drew was crying now, tears staining his face when he turned to look at her over his shoulder. "I'm sorry. I should never have said anything."

"The match hit my back and I screamed, knowing for sure this was the end. I cried out, begged her to stop, until I felt the fire burning into my skin. Then she cut me down, or the rope burned through, and I curled into a ball after rolling on the floor to put myself out. The doctors said it was the only thing that saved me. And as she tried to light me up again, to finish the job, her gown caught fire and she went up like a torch. The alcohol in her bloodstream and the can of fluid in her hand killed her within minutes."

He came to her then, not to comfort her, but to shake her hard. His fingers gripped deeply into her arms hard enough that she knew that she'd be wearing the marks for days. And when he let her go, shoved her from him, all she could do was stare at him.

"My mother haunts me. Not because she wants anything from me—no, that would be too easy to deal with—but because she thinks that I should be her little boy for the rest of my days. Rule me like she did when I was nothing. And even now, I'm nothing. She wants me there so that she can hate me like she has my entire life." He pulled his shirt off the bed and pulled it over his body, like a shield that she couldn't breach. "You won't have to be bothered with her again. I'll make sure that she understands that we are nothing to each other. I'm sorry you had to...you won't have to worry about her ever again."

Then he turned and left her, shutting the door behind him quietly, the door clicking loudly into place in the otherwise silent aftermath of the horror storm that she'd just witnessed.

Crumbling to the floor, she sat there, knowing on some level that she was going to hurt when she stood up, but also knowing that she didn't care. Her heart was broken. Not just for the man who had just left her, but for herself as well. Mac knew in that moment that when he'd stepped out of her room, he'd left her with a gaping hole where her heart had been.

As soon as she was able, Mac crawled to the bathroom and turned on the shower to its hottest setting. Getting in, she cried her heart out while the water moved over her, washing the tears that ran down her face hotter than the water was. Getting out, she dressed, packed her things, and called for a taxi. She and Rory were going home.

Drew

CHAPTER 6

"What are you going to do about the house?" Drew's first thought was to burn it to the ground, but he didn't say anything to Hugh. The man had been at his house when he'd gotten home last night, and hadn't left since. "I think you should hold onto it. This other job that you're going to, it might not work out."

"I told you, three times now, I don't have another job. I'm just leaving. I can't do this anymore." Hugh nodded and grinned.

Drew had called Steele as soon as he'd walked home and told him he quit. He told him that he was done, burned out, and needed to live his own life for a change. Steele had told him he'd talk to him in the morning and hung up. Drew had spent the rest of the evening telling Hugh what a fool he'd been. Not about quitting, but just in general. Especially about Mac.

"I don't think I can afford it anyway. The house, I mean. If you know of someone that wants it, sell it and give the money to some charity." Hugh only nodded again. "I hurt her, badly, and all she was doing was not taking any shit from me."

"Yeah, I can see where she might have been a little pissy with you and all. Even can understand why you told her

81

what had happened the way you did. Being in love can do the strangest things to you." Drew didn't even try to deny it. That was another thing that had occurred to him on his long walk home from Nick's house. He was in love with a near stranger. "You didn't tell her that part, did you, my man?"

"No. I was too busy being nasty to her because my dear mother showed herself to her." He thought of the dream he'd had of that night, the one where his mother had died. "I should call her and tell her I'm sorry."

"She left." Drew asked him how he knew. "Addie called me before I came over here to talk to you. Said she just called a cab and left. Taking her dog with her. She asked me to come here and kick your ass. But as soon as I saw you, I knew you'd done a fine job of that all on your own."

Drew nodded this time. He had too. And he might have done worse had he had something to do it with...ended his life as he'd thought about a lot over the years. He looked over at Hugh when he snorted. Drew wondered if he was making fun of him, but wasn't sure he really wanted to know.

"I think you should get a dog." Drew looked at Hugh and asked him why he'd do that. "You seemed to like having Rory around. He got you out of the house on occasion, and chicks love dogs. You could get a date or something."

"I don't want a date, or something. I want to be left alone." But the thought of a dog did sound good. "I'm going to move on, get my shit together, and keep my business to myself."

"You think that'll work for you? So you know, I don't think it will. You've had a taste of love, and it's not going to let you go so easily." Drew decided that having Hugh as a best friend wasn't all it was cracked up to be. The man was an annoying pain in the ass. And he really hated that he was nearly always right. "Or you could go out there where Mac is, tell her…nah, beg her, to forgive you for your stupidity, and live happily ever after."

"I can't do that, and we both know why." Hugh told him he didn't know anything like that. "And what if my mother comes back? No, not what if, but when she does. What do you suppose will happen when she comes back and tries to hurt Mac?"

"From what you said, I think that your mother might want to watch out for Mac. Mac is one scary woman if you ask me. And she had your back when you needed her, and stood up to your mother better than you ever did." Which was true. It didn't lessen his fear of what she'd to do Mac, but he thought she could hold her own with her. "And then there is the added fact that you are never going to be happy knowing that she's not in your life. Ever."

He wasn't now, and he was sure that Hugh was right. He wasn't going to be happy again. He'd had it great for a while, and now it was gone. He was going to be alone. Drew sat down and tried to think around the pain in his now empty chest. Eyeing his friend, he wondered to himself what Hugh would have done had he been in his shoes.

"What makes you such an authority about women and relationships? I've never known you to date a woman more than twice, you've never been in love that I know of, and you're as happy with a clingy woman as most people are a tax audit. Where are you getting your wealth of information?"

Hugh looked hurt. Sad too. But before he could tell him to forget it, Hugh sat down and started talking about her. The one…the one that had gotten away, he supposed.

"Her name was Kathryn. And I thought she had the most beautiful heart known to man." Drew sat very quietly as Hugh spoke. "I didn't just love her, but would have died for her. She

was my everything. Then she found out what I can do, and....
At first it was a joke for her, I think. Then as the weeks went
on, she began to get really interested in it. Always asking me
where they were, how many ghosts I could see at any time. It
took me almost a month to realize she was recording me. And
had it not been for a friend of mine who let me know, I might
have been committed to the padded room for the rest of my
life but for the fact that I can do a little magic myself when it
comes to computers. As it turned out she thought she could
'take care' of me and have power of attorney over all that I
owned. She wanted my home, my money, and.... And she
destroyed my heart. Which I'm pretty sure she didn't want in
the first place."

"I'm sorry." Hugh waved him off, but Drew felt bad for
him. "I don't think that Mac is like that. I mean, I'm pretty
sure that she's just as crazy as I am."

"Exactly right, my friend." Drew asked him what he
meant. "She's as nutty as you are. Hell, she might even be
a little more so than you. But she loves you. And you her.
Which brings me to this...go out there and get her. Have lots
of hot sex, and love her until you turn up your toes in death."

Alexandra fading into the room had them standing, both
of them afraid of her. Not of what she'd do to them, but she
sort of commanded one to honor her. Not with words, never
that, but with the way she presented herself. Drew had had to
work hard at not bowing before her when he'd first met her.
When she asked them both to have a seat, he nearly didn't
when she started pacing the room. Whatever had happened,
it wasn't good. Then he thought of Mac.

"Is she all right?" Alexandra told him she was. "Then
what is it? I don't know what might bring you out here at this
time of day, but it can't be good, can it?"

"No. I mean yes. Fuck." Drew glanced at Hugh when he laughed. "This is going to go badly for me, I just know it. When I asked her to help me I thought, what harm can come from this? I help my friends out, and you both live happily ever after. So what if that was going to be forever? You'd have each other, and what harm could — ?"

"Forever?" She turned to look at him as if she'd just realized what she'd said. "You said forever. That we would live forever. I'd like for you to explain that part to me, please. The rest of it too, but the forever part is a good place to start."

When she sat down, he did as well. He'd not even realized that he'd stood up until then. He could tell that Alexandra was trying to figure out how to tell him, so he asked for it straight up. Like a Band-Aid ripped off a wound.

"When she was in the hospital we didn't know what to do. I knew that the two of you were to be together, but her having the accident messed things up for you both. The timeline of your lives, so to speak. So I had to do something. Aster came to me then, and I told her what was going to happen. That because of her fall the two of you would never come together as a matched couple, and things would not be the same for either of you." He asked her what kind of things. "Mac would have died of an infection in three months, and you...you would have killed yourself when your mother drove you over the edge. You needed each other to survive, and more so, you need each other to help others of the world. A great many others."

"And how does that give them the ability to live forever?" Drew nodded at Hugh when he asked. It was a good question. "I mean, I'm thinking you helped her along. Gave her some of your blood to have her heal as fast as she did, didn't you?"

When she shook her head, he began to think that he didn't

want to know. But she spoke before he could tell her that he'd had enough for one day, thanks, and move on with his life. His apparently very long and boring life.

"Every vampire develops powers as they get older. For some it's the ability to be in the sunlight most of the day. Others have a gift that gives them insight on the lives of others. Then there are those that have the gift of life, which is what I have. Well, I have all three, but that's neither here nor there." She smiled and he felt his skin tighten. Her fangs were longer than he'd ever seen them. "I'm not going to hurt you, my dear boy. But you must know that I'm taking a chance in telling you this. But I digress, I only had to breathe into her mouth for her to heal and to give her long…longer life. And when you came together, you received the gift as well."

"I don't understand." Drew was pretty sure that Hugh did as well as he did, and he was afraid for it. "You mean that had they not had sex or whatever you meant when you said coming together, then she would have lived forever and Drew would have died? Not very sporting of you now, is it?"

"He loved her, and that was enough. But them having sex, it sort of sealed the deal, so to speak." Drew felt the walls closing in on him and tried to get the buzzing to stop, even if only for a minute. "Drew, you need her. Now more than ever."

Nodding, he went to the door and opened it to the outside. The air, fresh and a bit cold, blew over him and he felt a little better. Dealing with this, all of this, was going to be difficult, but it needed to be finished. Turning to her, he didn't move from where he was and asked what he needed to know.

"Why? And I don't mean why do I need her. But why did you do this to us? Why did you interfere into our lives and… and mess it up? I was happy before this. She was as well. Now we're in love because you meddled in our lives and gave us something that neither of us bargained for. Why?"

"Neither of you were happy. You certainly weren't. Even before this you were thinking that you'd had enough. That you were going to move on. She wasn't either. Not by a long shot." Alexandra stepped closer to him and he didn't back away, no matter how much he wanted to. "Tell me that you didn't think of ending your life daily before she came into your life. Tell me that the gun in your dresser drawer is only for protection. That you weren't picking it up nightly and putting it in your mouth. Tell me the truth, Andrew Ronald Mullins."

"I hated everyone and everything. But you still had no right." He thought he'd be hurt by the words he'd spoken aloud for the first time in his life. But he wasn't. It was... well, it was a relief. Something akin to having a heavy weight taken from him, if only for a little while. "Mac made me feel. Not just love, though if I was honest with you and myself, I never thought I'd ever feel that emotion. And I certainly never thought it would be given to me as she's done. Or at least I hope she has. My mother...she made me this way. And now that I've found someone that I'd very much like to love forever, she'll hurt her and us. I can't let her do that to Mac. Not for anything."

"If you don't go to her, love her as you should, then you both will end up isolated from the very people that would help you. Don't do this to either of you, Drew. You love her... go and tell her." Drew shook his head, but Alexandra held his head in her powerful grip. "You won't get another chance at happiness. Not ever."

"I can't." Before he could change his mind, he walked to the back door. It was well past time that he got on with his life.

Going to his car, he stared at Steele, who was leaning against his car like he'd been waiting on him. "Well fuck."

"Yeah, my thoughts exactly. Let's you and I talk."

He had no choice in the matter. Following Steele to the room he'd just left, Drew felt like he was going to be shot in front of a firing squad.

~~~

"I don't know why you're acting all sad. I'm the one that had the best sex in my life and fell in love with the idiot." Rory just whimpered at her and Mac knew just how he felt. "I can't help him if he doesn't want me to. You know that."

The dog offered no advice, nor did he tell her she was stupid. Which, Mac was pretty sure he thought she was. She'd been home for a whole two days now and she was lost. She didn't know where things were, the bed was too big, and she was afraid of the water that she had spent most of her life on.

"I can't believe I'm letting this thing get the better of me." Mac went to the big windows at the back of her house and looked out over the lazy river. "I'm standing here, terrified to go and do the things that I have loved all my life. I wonder if I can do anything like I did before."

She'd been an avid hiker, rock climber, as well as repelling off high places. Mac had skydived and done parasailing, as well as scuba diving. Her life was a series of adventures. Everything to the extreme...the reason she'd named her company that.

The knock at the front door had her standing still. It was going to be Olivia again, she just knew it. The woman was driving her crazy with this house. She was tempted to sell it to the first person that showed an interest in it just to get back at her. But the knocking persisted and she knew that she had no choice but to go and tell her once again she wasn't fucking selling. But seeing Landon there, a man that she'd only met briefly when she'd been at Addie's, wasn't what she had expected.

"Hey." She nodded at him. "I wanted to talk to you. Wow, this is a really pretty place. But I bet you know that. Can I come in?"

"What do you want, Landon?" He grinned at her and she wanted to hit him. The violence in her life now was starting to scare her. Every time someone spoke to her and it wasn't what she wanted to hear, she wanted to lash out. Preferably with a sharp object. "I'm not going to allow you to come in until you tell me what you want."

He moved by her and into the house. Rory came running at him and Mac smiled. But instead of barking and showing him that he didn't think he should be there either, the dog leapt at the man like he'd been starved for attention. And Landon was down on his knees talking to him and petting him like they were best buds.

"I have a list. I mean, I had a list. It's more like a book now. Every time my phone rang, someone was telling me to let you know about this or that." He stood up and turned to look at her with a stupid grin. "It's good to know what you're not fairing any better than Drew is. By the way, he doesn't know I'm here."

"Good for both of you. Hand me your book or whatever it is and get out." He pulled out a notepad and opened it up. "Look, Landon, I don't have time for this. I was going to...I was going to go out."

"No you weren't. You've not left your house since you've been back. And you stopped answering your phone too. Not very nice of you considering that you turned off the answering service and no one could talk to you. Sandy said that she has a ton of messages for you too." He pulled out a pen and checked something on his list before continuing. "Roger said to tell you thanks. He said that it's all cleared up now. Would you like to explain that one to me?"

"He was a guide for some really stupid people who thought kayaking down a river was meant to be a fashion statement. They got pissy with him when her very expensive shoes got wet." Landon pointed out that it was a river. "Yeah, go figure. You might get.... What the fuck do you want?"

"You to come home with me. Or short of that, now that I've seen your house, tell Drew to get his ass here and live happily ever after with you." She shook her head. "Didn't think that was going to work. But I did try. Any hoodles. He's not doing well."

Her heart ached to hear that. Well, she wasn't doing so well either. "He's a big boy. Tell him to see a doctor. I'm sure that he has one that'll help him."

"Not with this. He's leaving the team. Not that I blame him. Did you know that he was nearly burned alive by his mother?" She said nothing. "Ah, so you do know. And you ran because of what he looked like."

The slap was burning her hand before she even realized that she'd hit him. Landon stood there, a glint of humor in his eyes as he stared at her. The red patch on his cheek made her feel like shit, but he told her that it was fine.

"No it's not. Since I've gotten back home, all I want to do is hit someone." He rubbed his jaw. "What I want to do to people is well beyond a small hit to your cheek. I want...I need to hurt someone. Make them feel like I do right now."

"You love him." She told Landon that of course she did. "Then why are you here and he's...? Well, I'm really not sure where he is. Steele was going to try and make him stay, but I

90

doubt he was able to. Like you said, he's a big boy now."

"In the event you're guessing about what really happened, I'll tell you. His mother came to see him. And I interceded. Not well, I'm afraid, but I did. Then he showed me…he showed me what she'd done to him. Told me a nightmarish story about his birthday that I don't think I'll ever forget. Even if I wanted to." Landon nodded and she moved to the living room. There was no point in standing in the front hall like they were. "He's afraid of her, I think."

"He is. But not for the reasons you think. He's afraid of what she'll do to you. To any of us that he loves. That's why none of us knew about her. The woman never left her home after she died. Drew doesn't think she even knew that she could until the house was gone. The one that he lived in with her until recently." She asked him what happened to the house. "He sold it. And yesterday he finally got paid. It was a right tidy sum, if you ask me, but she had nowhere to go and looked for her son. The day that you encountered him was the first time she'd found him."

"She called me names." Landon told her he was sorry for that. "What did she do to him? I mean really? There has to be more than just the burn. Not that that's not bad enough, but I know there is more."

"There is. A great deal more. If you feed me, I'll tell you." She glared at him. "My wife thinks I'm charming and adorable. You're looking at me like I'm a bug on your shoe."

"I've met your wife, and I'm pretty sure that Dillon doesn't think you're charming either." He pouted at her. "That won't work either. I've made men like you cry in their wetsuit when a shark got too close."

"You do that? Swim with sharks?" She nodded and moved to the kitchen to see what was there. Mac knew there was food. Sandy had had groceries delivered, as well as a bunch of fresh fruit and vegetables. Her pantry was full. "I've never been much of an adventurous type. I like to bike and swim, but not with animals bigger than me. And certainly not in the way you have. I saw the pictures in your office."

Saying nothing, she fixed him a thick roast beef sandwich and gave him some carrot sticks. She didn't eat chips or any other snack food, but she did have a healthy appetite...at least she once did. After pouring him a glass of tea, she sat down at the bar with him and waited while he ate. Rory came in and stood by the door to be let out. Mac noticed that Olivia was coming toward her house, and she told Rory to go and jump on her. The dog took off like a shot.

"Not very neighborly of you. But Drew told me about her. She's got a real hard on to have your house, doesn't she?" Mac told him she was getting on her nerves. "I can see that. Why she wants it is something that I know too. Would you like to know why?"

"No. She's not getting it. End of story." But he only smiled and continued to eat his sandwich. "Oh all right, tell me. She said it was because she would use it better than me. She'd entertain, not leave it to ruin like I am. I don't know why she thinks she has any friends. Most of the people I've spoken to hate her as much as I do."

"She has plans to buy up all the houses along this route of the river. She and her partner have it in their head that there could be some money made here by putting up a hotel for the rich and stupid to use. And your little business — because from what I found out on her end, she does think Extreme is a one shot deal — is going to be run by you and your crew, but she'll see all the profits once she comes in and takes over. Mrs. Dutch is a ruthless bitch that thinks she's got it all together."

Mac was stunned. "It pays to know people that can be in an out of a person's home without them knowing."

"Ghosts." He nodded. "I see them now too. Not so much in my house, but on occasion they come by. Ignoring them doesn't work, does it?"

"No. They have this sort of sense when a person can see them. Most of them are harmless. A few…you've seen Adam, haven't you?"

"He wants me to die. Three times now he's…I didn't know they could take you. He's tried to get me to kill myself." Landon asked her how she'd been able to thwart him. "I'm stronger than he is. Both mentally and physically, I think. I kept telling myself that I didn't want to do this, and he finally had to leave me. Not that he hasn't tried again and again, but it's not so often now."

"It drains ghosts when they take you over. And the angrier they are, the more it takes away from them. You need Drew. He can help you. And in turn, you can help him with his mother. She's not going to give up until he's dead either." Mac nodded. "Good. I'll call him now."

It wasn't what she'd meant, but she didn't stop him from calling Drew. She was lonely. Sad and lonely, and wanted someone…. Mac had never been one to have a lot of people around her. She loved the things she did because they required you to be on your own for the most part. But the thought of having Drew with her, even for a little while, made her feel really good. For the first time in a long while.

CHAPTER 7

"I thought this rotation thing was supposed to be one week off and two on."

Steele didn't answer him. Drew really didn't care. He was leaving in the morning no matter how deep in shit they were. Looking out the window of the plane, he wondered idly what he was going to do with himself when he got to his new town. Mitch sitting down next to him had him groaning.

"No need for that. I'm not going to talk to you. You being the social animal that you are, I thought I could take a nap while we did this." Mitch closed his eyes and smiled. "Vinnie said to tell you that you're a fucking idiot, by the way."

He felt like he was as well, so he didn't comment. Twice now he'd started to call Mac and tell her what a fool he'd been, and both times he'd hung up the phone without connecting the call. She was better off without him, and the sad part of this whole thing was, she more than likely knew it.

"You really should stop feeling sorry for yourself." Mitch hadn't moved or opened his eyes when he spoke, but Drew asked him what he meant. "So melodramatic all the time, sighing heavily. Why don't you just go find her and tell her you're sorry? I tell Vinnie that every day at least twice."

"Because you're afraid of her." Mitch just laughed. "Not

to mention, you're afraid of her grandmother. Alexandra is scary if you ask me."

"But she loves me." There was that, Drew thought. "Also, you should know that I have a buyer for your house. And he's willing to pay the asking price for it too. I think there are plans to make it into some sort of shrine to you. You know, 'Whiney necro leaves here to find a new path and fails.'"

"Fuck you." Mitch laughed again. "Do you have a buyer, really? I mean…I only just signed the papers to have it shown this morning."

"No. I don't have anyone looking just yet. There is some interest in the land. The acreage is prime in our little area, but the house is just something that will more than likely be torn down if the right person buys it." Mitch looked at him. "I'm not taking any serious lookers until you get yourself settled. You never know, wherever you're going might not be what you wanted. I'm pretty sure that's a fact, because none of what you're doing involves you getting laid on a regular basis by Mac."

It wasn't going to be what he wanted, none of it was. What he wanted was in the opposite direction he was running to. Mac had been all he could think about since he'd realized he loved her with all his heart. Looking out the window again, he realized that he had no idea where they were going. Not to mention, not even what they'd be up against when they got there. But for the life of him, he really couldn't work up enough energy to even care. This was supposed to be his week off. And even though he was glad for the work, he didn't want to be nice to people. Living or dead.

When they were told to buckle up because they were about to land, he did so as did the rest of them. Flying had never really been his cup of tea when he'd first started working with

Steele and the rest of them, but now it was as easy as driving. As soon as they touched down and taxied their way to the hangar, he looked at the men he'd come with. They were all staring at him.

"What?"

He looked around as well, wondering not for the first time if his mother had come back. She'd been absent for the last couple of days, and he'd wondered if she was bothering someone else for a change. She didn't know anyone else but him, but perhaps he'd be lucky.

"You're going to hate us." Drew told Ray that wasn't even possible. "Yeah, well you might change your mind once you figure things out. Like the fact that there is no job to be had here."

"Figure things out? And what do you mean, there's no job?" He looked out the window again and it hit him where they were. "What have you done? Christ, have you lost your mind? She was safer with me gone from her life."

"No I wasn't." He looked up at the doorway to see Mac there. The rest of them left the plane, including the pilot. "Your mom showed up this morning. She has a real mouth on her, doesn't she?"

"I think she spent a lot of time on the docks. It might have been where I was conceived." It was a joke, one that he and Hugh shared a great deal when they were together. Mac didn't even smile, and he felt horrible for what he'd said. But she still wasn't safe being around him. No one was. "Why are you here? Or I guess, why am I here?"

"I need you in my life. I don't like being alone. And Rory misses you too. He's been moping around the house like someone took his favorite chew toy from him. The only time he gets excited is when I tell him to jump on Olivia Dutch. By

97

the way, she's suing me for breach of contract." He asked her for what. "I have no clue why she'd think so, but she has it in her head that I said I'd sell to her. And that my brother okayed it."

"Oh yeah, that would be me. But I didn't tell her anything but that you'd never sell." Mac came closer to him and he sat up in his seat. When she sat across from him, all he could think about was pulling her into his lap and kissing her. "She wants to buy all the places out around you. Did you know that?"

"Landon told me. He's very resourceful, isn't he?" Drew nodded. "I've missed you. I shouldn't have left you like I did. I think you might have missed me too. Just a little?"

"I love you. And I missed you a great deal." Her grin had him reaching for her and doing just what he wanted. Kissing her was like tasting for the first time, breathing in her scent was as if he'd never smelled before. Everything was new with her in his arms. Lifting his head, he looked at her. "I do love you."

"And I love you. But we have some things to work out." Nodding, he kissed her again. Then he moved her over his lap so that her legs were on either side of him. "You keep this up and we won't leave this plane for a while. And I have a nice big empty bed at my house."

"I need you." He pulled her shirt up and over her head. "Just a taste of you. That'll help me make it to your house."

When she unsnapped the front of her bra, he cupped both breasts in his hands and suckled at them, tasting the tips and nibbling on them until they were stone hard. Her breasts were warm, soft yet firm, and his. Sucking harder on them, he felt her riding him, and his cock hurt to be freed.

"Make me come." He nodded and lifted her up so that

she stood in front of him. Pulling down her shorts, he could see her arousal, even smell her need. Burying his nose into the dampness of her panties, Drew bit down on her and heard her cry out her release. "More. I need more."

Gladly, he thought as he pulled her panties off and slid his fingers into her. Sucking her clit now, he lapped at her juices as they filled his palm. Christ, he was never going to make it if she came like this. Flooding his mouth with her cream would make him come, he was sure. When she stepped back from him, he wanted to sob but she told him to strip.

Standing up now, he pulled his shirt off. When she took his own nipple into her mouth, he rocked his hard cock into her softness as she suckled at him. Drew wondered if it felt as good when he did it to her as it did when she sucked his nipple. Christ, he hoped so. It felt like heaven to him. Holding her to him, he worked his buttons free on his pants and freed himself. His cock was in her mouth before he could think what she was doing when she dropped to her knees in front of him.

Every time his cock disappeared into her mouth, he would surge forward. He loved watching her this way, his pants down around his knees, her mouth taking him like he wanted to her pussy. She cupped his balls now, holding them in her warm hand while she bobbed up and down on him. He was as close to coming as he'd been in a long while.

"I'm going to come. But I want to be inside of you first."

Her mouth left his cock and she licked the tip. It nearly sent him over the edge when she laid back and spread her legs for him. Tripping on his pants, he jerked them off and tossed them behind her as he settled between her thighs. Fisting his cock, Drew watched her hands tug and pull at her breasts. Sliding into her, Drew felt as if he were home.

"Fuck me, Drew. Fill me so I can scream out your name."

He slammed home again, pulling out to the tip and then filling her again. Each time he pounded into her, she held him tightly. Her fingers dug deep into his shoulder, her legs tightening around his thighs. When she came, crying out her release and then his name, he joined her, filling her hard and fast with every part of him. Christ, he thought as he dropped over her, he loved this woman more than he could have ever dreamed.

Rolling to his back and pulling her over him, he groaned when she sat up over him. As she rode him, slowly and fully, he watched her. Her face told him how much she was enjoying herself. As she tugged on her nipples, making them hard and pink, he wanted to sit up and suckle them again, but she told him to be still.

"I want to play." He asked her if she enjoyed playing by herself. "Sometimes. I have a vibrator that I use on occasion. But since I met you, it doesn't work as well. Do you suppose it's because I have you or that I need a new vibrator? Oh yes, that's it."

He slid his fingers into her pussy and felt his cock as she rode him. It was hot, erotic, and made him want more. But he had to slow them down or risk coming long before she did.

"Maybe I need to use it on you. That might make for some fun play as well." He could see her now, a vibrating dick at her pussy while he ate her. He surged upward when the thoughts turned more erotic. "I'd love to use it on you. Slide it into your pretty pussy while I sucked you. Maybe when I take you from behind, you could use it on yourself. I'd feel it, the vibrating against my cock while I'm in you."

"I'm coming."

Her scream of release startled him. He'd been watching her, and when the need to come had rolled over her, Drew thought her the most beautiful creature alive. Rolling her to her back, he took her once more, fucking her as hard as he could until he came again, bringing her twice more before he knew he was spent. This time when he rolled to his back, he closed his eyes and let sleep take him. He'd never been so relaxed before.

~~~

The house seemed alive now. Mac had left Rory in the house when she'd gone to the airport, and he was running around her and Drew like he'd missed them. Even scolding him to behave didn't slow him. She'd never realized how much an animal could become attached to a human before.

"He'll need to go out again if he keeps this up. I'm sure that he's not had this much energy since I got him." Drew laughed with her and Rory barked and ran around more. "Rory, wanna go and chase some bad guys?"

As he ran to the door, she moved too. Drew was right behind her, and when they saw Olivia in her yard, Drew pressed her against the now closed door and cupped her breasts. She was moaning even as Olivia watched them, her mouth hanging open like she was a fish on a hook. Before she could really enjoy herself, Drew turned her around and picked her up.

"I need to fuck you again. In a bed this time." Nodding, she wrapped her arms around his neck and held on.

The bedroom had never seemed so far away. When he put her on the bed and left her, she heard the door opening and closing and knew that he'd brought Rory into the house and put him in the living room. With a command to Rory to behave, Drew came back to the bedroom. She was going to be ready for him this time. Reaching into her bedside table, she pulled out her pink vibrator and turned it on. She was running it over her hard nipples when he was finally naked. His cock looked painfully hard, and she wanted it inside of her.

"Let me see you use it." She slid it down her body, pausing to run it over her navel twice as he watched her. "Slide it into you, Mac. Let me watch you come this way."

He had taken off his shirt, but he didn't turn around. He had done that on the plane too. Dressed without letting her see all of him. Sliding the dildo into her pussy, she told him to come to her. Even as he came to the bed, gliding like he knew just how sexy he was, he took off his pants and dropped them where they landed.

As he crawled up on the bed from the footboard, she knew he was enjoying her show. Every time the little feet on her vibrator got close to her clit, she moaned a little louder so he would know she was having fun. When his mouth joined her hand, Mac came, a small punch to her system that had her needing more.

"Roll to your belly. I want to fuck you that way." Moving the vibrator along her clit, she watched his face. "You're so wet right now. I could get my fill of you and you'd still be wet. Roll over love, I want to feel that thing on my dick."

She did as he said and felt him move up behind her as she got on her knees. It was hard for her to hold herself up and use the vibrator, so he took it from her. As soon as he entered her, filling her this way, Drew touched the now fast moving vibrator to her pussy and she came screaming. But he didn't stop, moving it firmer against her until she was dizzy with need. Even coming over and over like she was didn't fulfill her. It wasn't until he came, biting down on her shoulder as he released, that she felt it. Everything; sound, color, taste. All of it exploded around her until she simply let go.

When she woke up, laying in the middle of the bed, a blanket over her, Mac stretched and felt her muscles pull a little. Not as badly as they normally did when she was still for so long, but a little sore. Getting up, she headed to the shower and turned the water to hot. After brushing her teeth, she took a quick shower and went to her room. Drew was there with a tray in his hands.

"I thought you'd be hungry." Shy now, she nodded at him and wrapped the robe she'd pulled on in the bathroom around her. "I fed Rory and then took him for a long walk. He's a great dog."

"I know. The people I got him from said that they loved him, but couldn't keep him because of his unbounding energy. I think he was stuck in an apartment all day and had to figure out a way to make them understand he needed freedom too." Drew nodded and set the tray on the bed. "Are you going to join me?"

"I've eaten. It was...I didn't hurt you, did I?" Telling him no had her face heating up and she sat on the bed to see what he'd made. "I'm not the greatest cook in the world, but I can make a mean grilled cheese. I hope that's okay."

"It is. I love it." Picking up one half of the first of two, she bit down into the creamy cheese and moaned. "Oh, Drew, this is delicious. Can you cook anything else like this?"

"Pork chops, and I'm a pro at baked potatoes." He sat in the chair closest to the bed and watched her eat. "We have to talk. I mean...you need to know a few things before we talk about us."

"That we're immortal?" He looked surprised but nodded. "Aster came by yesterday and spilled the beans to me. I think she got some pressure from her brother to come and tell me. I guess we're going to be a long time on this world. But I think

103

we have things we need to deal with before they become too much. Like Adam Rush."

"My mother too. And Adam, like you said. Steele said he'd help both of us with them if we wanted him to." Mac ate the first sandwich, then picked up half of the second. "I think I'd like to try my hand at taking care of my mother alone. He said he wanted to be there, and I told him that was fine. If you want to know the truth, I'm more afraid of her than I am most everything else."

"I'll help you. I don't know what I can do, or can't for that matter, but I want to help." She finished off the half and played with the second part as she thought about what she needed to tell him. "You should know that I can't have children. An infection I had as a child messed things up for me. I'm okay with it, I guess. But, well, there's not a lot I can do about it now. But I'm looking into adopting Becky once she's able to leave the hospital. I would like for you to be okay with that."

"I can't have children either. My mother...she hurt me once and I can't reproduce. I think that was her plan. She certainly told me often enough that she hoped to Christ that I never had a kid like me." Mac knew that as well. There was a great deal of information to be had if you only knew how to look for it. Or knew a great hacker. "I quit working for Steele. I had to. I told him I'd help if he really needed me, but I'm not going to be doing it full time. Do you think you can find me a little bit to do around here?"

"Can you swim?" He told her that he could. "Then you're hired. Not for this season though. We're gearing down for fall. The water levels are too low this time of year to make it easy for boaters to go down the river. And it's dangerous as well. Falling trees and such. But if you want to learn how to snow ski, like long distances, we can get you geared up for that. And in the spring again, there is cliff climbing as well as repelling."

He laughed. "Do you ever stop?" She smiled at him as she finished up the sandwich and leaned back against the headboard. "I want to stay here with you. Actually, I've been thinking, and if you'll have me, I'd like to marry you."

"I'd like that." He nodded but didn't move. "What else aren't you telling me, Drew? If we're going to make this work, and we have a long time to spend together, we need to be honest and not keep things from each other."

"All right." He sat there for several minutes and she let him. Whatever was bothering him he was really worried about it. "My mother, you know that she comes to me. I mean, you've seen firsthand what sort of person she is. She's not much different than she was when she was alive."

When he didn't continue, she spoke. "My mother died when I was born. Nothing to do with me, but she'd been sick before she'd conceived me, and having me put a strain on her heart that killed her a couple of days after I was born. My father was my world. He was both mother and father to me my entire life. When I would go out for a sport, it didn't matter what it was, he was right there cheering me on. And when I decided to open Extreme, this one, he gave me the money to do it. I paid him back in a year. Then he was killed when he entered a grocery store at the wrong time. I miss him every day."

"My mother didn't want me. She told me that daily. Even told me most days that she hated me. Once she hired a man to murder me, but I was able to get some help from the people that I help and she didn't succeed. Or he didn't, I guess. Several days later the man killed himself and my mother blamed me." Drew leaned back in his seat, but she knew he was far from

105

relaxed. "I don't think you could call my life a normal one."

Nodding, she knew that too. His mother had gone to the police and told them that her son had murdered a man before he could in turn murder her son. The police had had dealings with her before, a drug addict as well as a general prostitute, so they had written it off as the ramblings of a woman off her meds. It wasn't until the body showed up some weeks later that they'd gone to talk to her, and by then she was dead. And Drew was in intensive care at the hospital for the injuries that he'd gotten when she'd set fire to them both.

"Did your friends help you out?" He nodded but didn't elaborate. "Adam is, as I said, coming around more and more often. What can we do to stop him from hurting me and you? I'm assuming that he won't just stop with hurting me now. I told Landon about it, how he moves into my body and tries to get me to kill myself. I don't want that to happen."

"Neither do I. And now that we can't die...I'm not sure how that really works yet, but I told Alexandra that we'd need to have some lessons in caring for ourselves after a bit." Mac told him she thought that was a good idea. "When he comes into you, how do you feel? I mean, do you know that he's there or not?"

"Yes. I can...it's like I have this growth in me. Silly I know, but that's what it feels like. And I get really sick when he leaves me. I mean, puking my guts up sick." She asked him if that was normal.

"No. Well, yes. It's not normal that you can feel him, but that might be because you weren't born this way. As for the being sick, that's from his thoughts and emotions. His anger, if you will. It leaves a sort of residue behind when he is gone, and because you're not like him, it makes you ill." Mac thought that made sense. He was a pretty pissed off man. "Have you talked to his wife yet?"

"Cindy? Yes. A couple of times. She had a rough life. And I had no idea he was the one that knocked me into the falls, did you?" He told her that he'd seen the cam that she'd had on her. "I haven't. I'm not sure I'd want to either. Just give me the highlights if you don't mind."

"When you called for help, Sandy turned the flooders, as she called them, on you. I guess you have cameras all along the route you go down when you have clients." She nodded. The insurance company loved that addition, and it had saved her ass a couple of times when a customer had claimed that she'd left them on their own. "With your camera, they've been able to piece together what happened. When you rescued Becky, pulled her up from the water, her father hit the back of your kayak with his body, trying to dislodge the two of you. They weren't sure at first what it was he used, but they found pieces of wood in the kayak that came from a piece of log. He knocked the two of you over on purpose. It is thought that he was trying to save himself by taking the boat. I don't think he counted on needing to be able to use it if he ever got in it."

"He wanted me to save him first. When he came to me once, he even said that he could have had another kid if Becky had drowned, but now that I'd let him die, murdered him, there would be no more. I don't think he would have been happy with any outcome. Other than the one where he came out on top. And like I said, he would have found some reason to bitch about it not being right." Picking the tray up, she made her way to the kitchen. The lights were soft in there, and the entire room was bathed in moonlight from the overhead skylights. "I couldn't have let her die. You know that, don't you?"

"Yes. I wouldn't have either. In my job, my former job,

107

we would see the destruction of children all the time. Mostly by the people who were supposed to care for them. When we could save one, even if they were hurt more than they should have been, it was a real victory for us. A feeling that we were doing something right." Drew took her into his arms. "We'll take care of Adam first. Then we'll tackle my mother. If we need help, we can call in the big guns, but I think together we can make them leave us alone."

She had no idea why, but she didn't think it was going to be that easy. Neither of them, his mother or her tormentor, seemed the type to give up easily. Holding onto Drew, she knew that if push came to shove, she'd call the big guns herself and banish them. A term she'd learned from Constance.

Mac wondered if Drew had any idea how many people loved him, and were willing to help him in any endeavor. She was going to have to think of a way to pay them all back too. Maybe a nice sedate fishing trip one day. Where everyone stayed in the boat and caught fish big enough to have for dinner.

CHAPTER 8

Where was he? Everywhere she looked, Belinda could not find her son. The ungrateful little bastard had better not be hiding from her again. She was getting really sick of his crap. Maybe she'd have to teach him another valuable lesson in remembering his place.

Thoughts flittered through her mind then. Fire. Pain. And something else that she couldn't hold on to. There had been screaming too. Whether it was hers or the boy's she wasn't really sure, but she knew that something wonderful had happened, and something so terrible that she didn't want to think about it. Looking around again where her home had been, she wondered if he'd done that to her too.

"If he thinks that tearing down my house to where I can't stay there will keep him out of the whipping bed, then he's dumber than I thought." But he wasn't. Andrew was smart, too smart for his own good most of the time. He wasn't fun either, and hadn't been for a very long time. "Never wanted to get high with me. Didn't even want to go out and get me some shit either. What kind of kid leaves their mother hanging like that? Him. That's who."

Belinda knew that she'd hurt him. It didn't really bother her overly much, except when he couldn't go out and score for her. Not that she was a drug addict or anything like that. It just helped when her sadness took her really deep. Of course, that did happen more and more after he came along. And even when he couldn't get out and help his poor mother, she'd beaten him until he did it anyway. The one time he'd passed out and ended up in the emergency room, she'd thought she'd die before he got his ass home. Nearly sent him back there, too, she'd been so pissed off at him. A thought, a pain of something was right there. Then it was gone again, another little blip that told her that she'd missed some sort of information. Information that was vital to her. She didn't want to think about things that made her head hurt like that. Instead, she thought of that boy.

"This is all his doing. Leaving me like he did. I'm the one that says we're done. And I ain't done with him. Not by a long shot. What the hell does he think is going to happen to my check every month? I can't live without that money coming in. It's not like he ever gave me any money…and I know he has it, too."

She moved down the long row of large equipment that had shown up several days ago. Her house, along with four others, was now rubble on the ground. One of them big scooper things had picked up most of it, but had stopped when she'd shown up. Belinda wanted to think it was because of her, but she knew it was quitting time. Nobody worked hard anymore. Not when they could get something for nothing.

"Like I do," she said with a laugh. "That's why I didn't get rid of that boy of mine when I could have. Like them others that came along, he should have been in the dumpster too. But I waited a little too long for that one. Them jailers, they made me late for my abortion." Belinda was slightly bothered that she was talking to herself. But since this thing with the boy had happened, she didn't have anyone else to spout off to.

When he'd been born, Belinda had actually considered smothering the thing. While she lay there in that little bitty bed at the hospital, she thought how much effort it would have cost her to do it. Of course them nurses didn't treat her right, telling her that she had to care for him, change his shitty diapers…even wanted her to let him suckle at her breast. Like that was ever going to happen. She wasn't going to get saggy tits because she'd had the misfortune of getting herself knocked up.

Then one of them welfare women came in to see her; had a nice briefcase and pretty dress on, like she was something. Belinda had seen her kind before. They turned their nose up at people like her. The ones trying to get as much as they could before they left this world.

"Miss Mullins? I'm here to help you out with the paperwork for your food card." Belinda looked over at the bassinet and so did the woman. "He's a healthy fine boy, and will bring you much joy in your golden years. You'll need to take better care of yourself if you want to keep him. The county doesn't want to have to take him from you, and I'm sure you don't want that to happen either, do you?"

It had been on the tip of her tongue to tell her she didn't want him anyway when the women took out her clipboard. She started naming off the things she'd be getting now that she had a boy, and the rules she'd have to follow to continue getting them.

"You'll have an extra six hundred and seventy-three dollars a month to help pay for his formula and such while he's an infant. You'll also get a check to purchase his diapers and other things that a newborn will need. A crib has been donated to you, as well as a layette set for him, to help you get started on being a mother. Then as he gets older, you'll get more to help with that. Growing boys need to eat well, don't you think?" Belinda nodded. She only got two hundred a month now…this was going to be a lot better. "Also, because of the new program that the state is in, you'll get to live in the house that you're in and we'll help you with the rent and utilities. Do you have a cell phone?"

She didn't and told the woman that she couldn't afford one. The lady went on to tell her that she'd need to have a phone with a baby in the house, and made two calls on hers. Twenty minutes later, not only was there a new phone there for her, but she had a credit card, one of them one time user things, to get herself a case to put it in.

She didn't of course. That money went right to her dealer. And with that, most of her first month of food money. Buying the shit that they had on the list for the brat was too expensive, so she cut corners with that by adding some of the powdered milk that she got at the free food place. All in all, having the brat around was paying off more than she'd ever dreamed.

When school started up for him, there was more money and food than she could have spent in one day. She tried, too. And clothes. Everyone had something to hand down or out to her for the kid. Even as he got older, the money kept pouring in, even when she'd had enough of his ways. Especially when he thought he should have something for his fucking birthday.

"Damned kid was becoming a pain in the ass." He'd been on her all that week about his birthday. All he'd wanted was to have enough money for a pizza. She liked pizza well enough, but not a hot one delivered to the door. She was more into selling herself for a little sausage, and getting a good deal more than the kind that might have been on it. And when she'd told him she'd trade deals with him, he had the nerve to ask her what her end of the bargain would be before he would agree to anything. Smart assed punk had the nerve to question her.

Her head started to buzz again. It did that whenever she thought of pizza. Even seeing others eating it, she felt like there was something on her, clawing at her. Moving away from the big equipment, she let whatever was making her feel poorly move on back away from her head and out. She was dealing with it as best she could until her boy could help her out. She needed a score worse than she ever had before.

"He's gone and seen that woman again. I told him to stay away from her. I must have told him a dozen times. Does he listen? Hell no. Time to teach him another lesson, I guess." The woman, the whore, had been sleeping with her kid, and that wasn't right. A pain in her head had her pausing in her walk to hold onto something, but she missed it and felt herself swaying on her feet as things went from bad to worse. As the thoughts of the woman grew stronger, so did the pain in her head. "I'm going to hurt her, that's what I'm going to do. She won't touch anything that belongs to me again. And he's going to pay too. First for not listening to me, and then again for thinking he's too big for his britches. I'll beat them right off him before I let him think he can get away with this."

Christ, she hated that kid. And everything about him. There had been times, when she was feeling pretty low and pissed at him, that she'd picked up the phone to have him taken care of. Shivering when she thought of what them social people might have done to her, she always laid the phone back down. But he got a worse beating for her cowardice.

Belinda could have sold off her boy a few times when he'd been younger, to men who liked to fuck little boys. But she had her principles. If she couldn't get any, he wasn't either. And the few times she'd been tempted to just let them have him, something always got in the way. Something pushed at her head and she just couldn't do it without some pain. It hurt her like a mother fucker too. Money, she'd been told, would have made her rich if she could just let him go. But someone wouldn't let her.

"Couldn't." And she still had no idea why she'd not just done it other than listening to the fucking woman. A voice, some bitch, had gotten into her head and told her that she'd die if she did it. And when she showed Belinda how she'd die, a horrible and painful death, Belinda decided that it wasn't worth the money from selling him off if she had to go through that.

"Andrew Mullins, where the fuck are you, boy? I'm telling you right now that it ain't gonna go well for you when I find you." He was not really a boy, she supposed. At some point, and she had no clue when it had happened, he'd become a man. A big scary man really. And he could do things now, things that no boy of hers should have been able to do. He could fix things. Not just broken things like had forever been around the house when he'd been little, but also his clothing. He did the laundry. Made his bed. She'd even made fun of him when she'd seen him vacuuming the floor a few times. She let him…the welfare people had a way of just popping in when she didn't want them to. All the while she had been sitting on the couch watching television, he would just try to keep things working and in order. She kind of hated that about him too.

"No. Not sitting. I'd been…something. I'd been doing something else. Probably getting high again. I loved that feeling of being high."

It was times like this that Belinda needed to lie down. Her head was making her sick again and her body was hot. Hotter than it had been when she burned her fingers cooking some wieners over the gas stove. The stick she'd been using caught and burned all the way to her fingers before the wiener was even close to being done. "I'm guessing that wasn't really his fault, but I sure did blame him for it."

Closing her eyes, she thought of her boy and all the things she was going to do to him when she got to him. And when she opened them, she was standing outside a big log house. The water running close beside her had her thinking of the television shows where they did those nature things, but she moved away from it all together. She didn't care for water and only bathed in it when she had to.

The dog coming at her nearly had her screaming. "Go away, you stupid dog, before I cook you up for my dinner." He growled at her, not just showing his big teeth, but his fur standing up on end too. "Get now. I don't want to have to hurt you."

But his barking and growling had the lights coming on in the house. Before she could make her way back to the trees behind her, the woman stepped out and whistled. It was the whore.

Taking a step toward her, Belinda knocked against something hard. Putting out her hands to see what it was that was stopping her, it burned into her and had her jumping back. She couldn't see anything, and the longer she stood there glaring through the wall and at the woman, the madder she got.

Then her boy walked out onto the porch. She was sure he could see her. In fact, she was positive of it when he crossed his arms over his chest and glared right back at her. The boy was going to pay for that, for sure. He was getting mighty uppity for someone that needed her.

"Come on out here and get yourself home. I've been looking for you for weeks now, and you just about tried my patience to the limit. You heard me, get your ass over here and take me someplace to live." He just stared at her. "I know you can hear me, boy. Come out here now or so help me, you'll pay for this. You're gonna anyway, but you might be able to walk after if you do as you're told."

"I don't think so. I'm my own man now, and I'm not your whipping boy any longer. You never liked me in the first place, so now you have the chance to get free of me. And even if you don't, you're not going to bother us again." She'd see about that and moved toward him again, completely forgetting about the wall. This time she felt the burn all over her front and back. She patted at her clothing and skin to put out whatever burning was there when her boy laughed at her. "You won't be able to come near this house nor those in it, Mother. I've had a friend of mine put a protection around this house and property. I want you to go away and leave us alone. Or else."

"Or else what, boy? I'm not afraid of you or your so called friends. You got yourself a taste of pussy now and you think you can treat me the way you want? Nope, not going to happen. You can't be doing that to me. I'm your mother." The heat surrounded her. She could feel it all over her and it made her wish she'd stayed close to the water. "Come on out here, Andrew, and we'll go on home. I won't beat you much for treating me this way. But you've done this all on your own."

Instead of answering her or doing what she told him to do, he pulled the woman into his arms and took them both into the house. Even the fucking dog went with them. Belinda was furious now. Moving again to the wall, her body hit it hard, this time knocking her back hard enough that she landed into a pile of trash and rubbish. It took her a minute to realize that she'd landed in her old house. The one that had been destroyed when her boy had left her.

~~~

Her hands were still shaking and Drew wanted to tell her that it was going to be all right, but he knew they were hollow words to her right now. Mac put down her teacup when most of it sloshed over the sides. And when she looked at him, he could see the worry and fear there. Not that he blamed her... he was a little scared himself.

"Tell me again why she wasn't able to come up to where we were? I was a little freaked out earlier when I saw her in the neighbor's yard. So I don't think I got the entire story behind that. You said protection." He opened his mouth to answer her but she put her hands up. "Never mind. I don't think I'll be able to understand you anymore now than I did the first time. Just tell me she can't come in."

"She can't come in. Neither she nor Adam can breach the magic surrounding this house, thanks to Steele." She nodded and picked up her teacup, only to set it back down again. "On a different note, Rory can see her too. Did you know that?"

"No. And I don't think I can handle you explaining that to me either. We'll just bank that for later when I'm feeling less like a rabbit falling down a hole. A deep one. Without a ladder. Or net." He was glad, to be honest...he wasn't really sure why the dog had seen her. Drew had heard that animals could see the dead, but never had any proof of it until now. It was on his growing list to ask someone about. "You called the others?"

"Yes. Steele said that he and Kari will be here as soon as

117

they're able. They're bringing the baby, so you know. Landon is close. He's just turning his car around and coming to us. He'll be here first, unless his wife materializes before he gets here. So Vinnie will be here soon. I want to warn you that she won't be coming by car. You understand that, right?" Mac nodded. "Alexandra is on her way too. In fact, she's in the basement. She said she'd come up when you were better."

"You think I will be?" He smiled at her. "Don't be charming, Drew. We have a dead woman on our front lawn making threats to us. Another ghost trying to take my body so that he can make me slit my wrists. So I'm pretty sure that if you continue to be nice and calm, I might just have to hurt you."

"I love you." She growled at him and he laughed. He just couldn't seem to help himself. He was afraid, horrified of his mother for coming like she had, but he had Mac and he was about as happy as a man could be. "And we'll get through this. All of it, and come up smelling like a pretty rose. You'll see."

"What could she possibly want? I mean, really. She's dead. So what could she want with you?" He told her that he wasn't sure she knew she was dead. "Excuse me? How is that possible? Didn't she burn up? I'm not sure, but I'd think that would make a lasting impression on someone. Even when I burn my finger, I know it."

"Yes. But I don't think she's let it sink in that she's actually dead. Or maybe she just simply doesn't believe it. I mean, I never mentioned it to her and she never brought it up. Only to tell me that she wanted to kill me. I never realized until now that she might have it in her head that she is alive. Or something like that. It happens to some people who simply think that they're going to live forever, or that they're much too young or smart to be killed. You know the type, they eat pine nuts and drink gallons of water." He was going for humor and it failed big time if her face was any indication. "She died a traumatic death. And most of the time they block it out. I'm not sure how they can do that, but once they remember what caused their deaths, they usually go away nicely."

"Do you think your mother will do that? Decide to play nicely once she finds out she's dead?" He shook his head. "I see. Drew, the next time I ask you a question like that, I'd prefer that you lie to me please."

"You don't want me to do that. And I don't want to. You ask me a question and you have to want the answer. The right one." He watched her face as she tried to work this through. It was a lot to take in. It was for him most of the time too. "I'm really sorry."

"Thank you, but I'm not. Not really. Now we know that she's found us. As much as I hate having her around, I know that she can't get to us so long as we're here, and she won't be able to hurt you either." He didn't say anything. "Drew, you said you'd not lie to me. What is it now?"

"We can't stay here forever. Life has to go on, and we can't hide out here in this house. You know that."

Nodding, she got up and put her teacup in the sink and reached above her head and pulled down a bottle of bourbon. He wasn't sure that was such a good idea, but said nothing as she poured about two fingers of it into a glass. When she offered it to him, he declined. Drew did not drink. As she played with the still full glass, he knew she was thinking about all the possibilities that could happen should they stay hidden here. None of them would work. Not now and not for them.

"What can she do to us? I mean, tell me like you don't love me." He didn't want to, but he knew that if she was ready, she'd be safer. "Please?"

"Torment us until we can't take it anymore. Invade our dreams, if she were able to get to us. Whisper in our ears, tell us to do things that we would never do on our own. She can take the body of someone and have them kill us as well, as you have noticed. Whatever she needs them to do, no matter the cost to the person, she can control them." Mac asked him what it would cost the person. "If they're not moral and are corrupt, nothing much other than a sick belly and a headache. Some, I've heard, get a rush out of it...the living, I mean. If they're not mean or they abhor killing of any kind, she could drive them insane, even to the point where they might end their life. Any ghost that takes a living person has consequences too. They're drained for a time. And what they have them do and for how long will determine the length of rest they'll need before they can come back for more."

"Adam would take me, and the harder I fought him, the longer he would have to rest up. I get it. Can they be drained fully? Like a gas tank can?" He said that it didn't work that way. "Then how the hell do you get rid of them if they keep bouncing back every time you knock them down? You know, I think I liked it better when I didn't know there were ghosts and other things that could hurt you. I would have been perfectly happy just living my life like a regular normal person. How do we get rid of them?"

"We have to banish them." He hated to think of doing that to his mother. No matter what she'd done to him in the past, she was his mother. But if she harmed Mac or any of the others, all bets were off.

"What does that mean?" He told her that he wasn't really sure, he wasn't able to do it. "But someone can, right? One of the men and women you work with, they can do it."

"Yes. Steele can. Addie as well. I think even Nick can, but I've never seen him do it." She asked him if it was painful to the ghost. "It destroys them. Everything about them. They become nothing. No afterlife if there is one. Nothing but the memories of the people that they left behind. Nick told me once that other ghosts, ones he thought were assigned to help us, take them and.... He told me that they tear them apart, quite literally."

She was quiet then. Drew didn't know what was going on in her mind, but he knew that whatever happened from now on, she was going to be a part of it. In dealing with his mother and Adam. If they were ever going to be able to live out their lives, it was going to be because they both took a stand against these people.

"I'm sorry, Drew. I had no idea. I can see where you'd not want to do that. I mean...she's a royal pain in the ass and she did hurt you, but to get rid of her would tear me up too if she was my mom. But I'm telling you right now, if she hurts you or tries to take you from me, I'm going to have her banished right out of our lives. No holds barred."

"Good." Mac sat on his lap after pouring the untouched bourbon down the sink. He was glad for that. He knew that having a crutch, liquor in this case, would not be a good thing. And he hated the taste of it anyway. "When they get here, we're going to have a houseful. Are you ready for that?"

"Yes. Christ, I've lived here for so long all by myself and my dog. No one bothered us, we just went about our business." She turned on his lap and kissed him. "Now, with all this, I have to say I kinda like having people around. The living, not the dead."

Steele and Kari arrived with little Aster in tow about an hour after Landon did. Nick and Mitch came with pizza and beer when Vinnie arrived and went to talk to her grandmother. Hugh brought his laptop and the video from the river accident for anyone to see if they wanted. Mac had a feeling that at some point, she was going to have to look at what they had. Dillon had to lie down for a bit—the baby was making her tired all the time—and Addie dozed on the couch as they sat around after pigging out on the food. After a while, Steele brought up the recordings.

"I'm not sure I'm ready to watch this."

No one said a word to Mac. If he was honest with himself, he wasn't sure he wanted her to see it either. It was sickening how the camera caught everything, every bob in the water, every rock that she hit, the blood that appeared on the lens just as it went still. And the little girl, Becky's, foot, that didn't move until the camera went black.

"I'd like for you to see it up until the point where you went down. All we have is the video from your head cam, so I'm not sure how much you'll be able to see anyway." Mac looked at Drew when Steele continued. "I need for you to tell us if the boat slipped from you or if you were pushed. I know what we saw on the other cameras, but it's not one hundred percent clear that Adam did what he was accused of."

"You mean knocking the boat free of the rocks?" Steele nodded when Mac looked at him. "His wife, she said that he did it too. What does it matter now how we ended up in the falls? I mean, we're both alive thanks to some magic. What difference does it make if a dead man tried to kill us?"

"There's a lawsuit against your business that says you were responsible for their deaths. From the family it says, but after looking into it deeper we found out who it was. There is no one but Becky that we can find, but some lawyer got a burr up his ass and is suing on her behalf. If we can show that the father did this to her and caused his own demise, and that of his wife in the process, then the lawsuit will go away. He won't have anything to stand on." Mac said that she didn't care about that. "But Becky will. If it comes out later, if she hears that you might have been at fault, then she'll resent you. And you don't want that anymore than the rest of us do. This is better for all of you. Especially if you go through with the adoption."

"I am. We are." Mac nodded once, as if she'd come to a decision. "Which camera angles do you have? I mean, where did you get your other recordings from? The office ones too?"

"I don't know what you mean. It's the same ones that were given to the police from your office. It was the one from the cameras that Sandy gave to them. And the video from the one on your head seat." She asked him about the one on her vest. "Vest? No. I don't think anyone was aware there.... Do you have it now?"

"Sure. I have them all. I mean, from the time I put them in until.... Well, if someone puts on a vest, and everyone is required to, we start the recording. It works off the snaps on the vest. When it's locked, they turn on." Steele asked her if the couple had one. "No. They weren't a part of my work. I have mine of the entire day. Would you like to see them?"

They all followed her to the lower levels. Drew had not been down there as yet and was surprised by the large fire room, as she called it, that housed not just the computer system that pretty much scanned the entire fifteen miles of the river she used, but around her house as well. After she showed Steele and the others how to pull them up, Mac asked to speak to Drew in private. He followed her back up the stairs to their room.

CHAPTER 9

Mac moved along the corridors to the room that they'd transferred Becky to that morning. Her lawyer had called and told her pretty much what Steele had said about the guy who was supposed to be representing Becky. But he also told her that the man did not have a leg to stand on when it came to suing her for the death of Becky's parents. She was glad now that Steele and the others had stayed over last night. She might yet need them.

"There's this attorney that's saying that you neglected to let anyone know about the currents and their strength. First of all, I'm not sure how this guy thinks that you had to tell him when he was not your client, and he owned a house close to the river too. And secondly I don't think he realizes how many signs you had put up a few years back telling anyone and everyone about Winding Falls." Not only had Mac hung the signs, but she'd also made sure that each dock in the water had a sign posted on it to assure that anyone passing by on their own watercraft knew. The city had approved it when they realized two things...she wasn't going to go away until they did just what she wanted, and they weren't going to have to maintain or pay for them. "Also, he has it in his head that you encouraged them to swim in the waters that were dangerous. This man is not going to play nicely, I don't think. But what he fails to realize, as most people do, is that you are not stupid, nor are you one to back down from a challenge."

"Thank you, I think. I have to make sure this goes well, Roger. I want to make sure that little girl is taken care of, and I can do it." That was what she had needed to talk to Drew about. She wanted to ask him if he was all right with adopting the little girl. "You should know that I'm getting married soon too. So we'll need to get together and make sure that my new husband has what I have."

"Congratulations. And we can do that starting now if you want. I can have all the papers drawn up and his name put there for you. Then all you have to do is say the 'I dos' and let me know." She asked him if he could make it for next week and gave him all the information she had on Drew. "I don't know what he has other than the things he brought with him. I think he has a house."

"Let me see what I can find out about him online. He does. It's...shit, Mac. He owns the Logan mansion. Do you know who his lawyer is?" She told him the guy's name. Mac had gotten a great deal of that sort of information from Drew while the rest of them looked at the camera angles that she had. "I'd not wait too long if I were you on getting things settled. This other guy, he's moving forward like it's his job to have you broke and sitting in a jail cell for murder. Have Drew call me as soon as you can. And I'll get things set up for after the nuptials."

"We're in town on other business. Can we come by now? That way we can get it over with and you can move on with anything you might need to." He said that he'd open her a slot even if he had to say he was sick. "You don't have to do that, but please see what you can do."

And now, after the lengthy conversation with her attorney on the phone, Mac and Drew were at the hospital to talk to Becky. Mac looked at Drew before they moved into the room. He smiled at her and kissed her quickly on the nose.

"I don't know what we'll find in there. I mean, her dad could be here, or just her mom." Drew said that it was just her mom. "And how do you know that?"

"I have had someone watching over them both for a few days. Donny is a friend of the team and he's.... You should know that he's sort of sweet on you. He is just a kid so he's sort of fickle on who he loves at any given moment, but he does like Becky and has been talking to her a lot when her mom's not there. I think he might have even told her about you and me, as well as her coming to live with us." Mac had a lot to learn about this ghost business. "Her father hasn't been to see her since she's been here. Just the mom."

"She wants me to adopt her daughter too, did I tell you that?" He said that she had. "And did I tell you that I love you today?"

"You have, but I can never get enough of hearing you say it. I love you as well. And so you know, Kari has pulled a few strings, and our marriage license has been approved. I think the women are getting things ready for us to be married tomorrow if they have anything to say about it." She nodded and he smiled at her. "You still want to be my wife, don't you?"

"Of course. But we'll have to go and talk to Roger after this. I want everything all tied up neatly before things go much further." He asked her what. "I'm wealthy. I mean...I have a shit ton more money than I could spend in a lot of lifetimes. And you get it too."

"I don't want your money, Mac. I'm just—" She cut him

off, telling him it didn't work that way. "I have some money as well. Not a shit ton, but enough to live on should you never want to work again. Not that I think that would be possible even if you didn't have Extreme. You get what I have as well. We share everything, all right?"

"Deal." She looked at the still closed door. "I hope he's in there. I mean, I know that he wants to hurt me, but I'd really like to get this crap over with so we can move on with other important things. Like making love. That's important, isn't it?"

"Very much so." Drew pulled her into his arms and kissed her. When he let her go, she had to hold onto him for several seconds while her heart got back under a normal pace. When she looked up at him, he grinned at her. "I don't want you to ever think I don't love you."

He opened the door and gave her a gentle push inside. Cindy was there, standing by the bed of her little girl, and Becky was talking to her. As soon as she saw them, Becky smiled and told her what her mom was saying.

"She said that I can go with you when I leave here." Mac nodded and looked over at Cindy when Becky sounded so excited. The last thing she wanted to do was to hurt the other woman. "And Mom said that she can see me when I want. Not all the time because she's not here anymore, but I can call out to her and she'll come if she can."

Her and Drew had talked about Becky being able to see ghosts. They had no idea if she had come close to death that day in the water. Nor did either of them know if Becky would continue to see her mother long after she reached that point in her life when she grew out of such things. Most children could communicate with the dead, but at about ten or so, they either lost interest or the ability to do so. Either way, they had to wait on Becky to grow up to be sure. They also cautioned her about telling others that she could see them. Adults for the most part did not want to think about ghosts or have someone, a child especially, telling them what they were saying.

"I wanted her to be ready, so I thought I'd have a little talk with her about you and what is going to happen. I've explained to her that I'm no longer going to be able to care for her due to the accident, and that she'd go with you to get all the care she needed. And love. You will love her for me, won't you?" Mac told her that she already did, but appreciated all the help they could get in this. "I also told her that she'd be happy with you as well. And that her daddy wouldn't be there. I think she understands more than I thought she did about her father's and my relationship."

"I think that's the way most parents feel after a time. But I promise you, she'll be safe from him. Have you seen him lately?" Cindy said that she'd not been looking for him and he'd not been by to see their daughter. "He's been at my house until recently. He can't get in there again. We've taken precautions against that."

"Mr. Bennett and his group." It still amazed Mac that so many of the living challenged, as she'd been calling them, knew who the Bennetts were and the men that worked with him. Even Drew was well known and respected among them, and she felt proud to be a part of what he did. Even if it was just on the sidelines, where she wanted to stay. She didn't know if she'd go and work with them on jobs, but she was glad that they'd been there for her. "I've been talking to an older gentlemen named Carlton. I think that Ray sent him to see me. He's been helping me learn what I need to do to keep Adam from coming here and hurting anyone. He was never a good man when he was alive, and he's gotten worse now that he's dead. I think he believes there are no consequences for his actions."

"There are. For each problem he causes to the living, if done with purpose and malice, he has to pay for it. Some get years added onto their sentence for how long they have to stay here on this earth. Others, like your husband, he'll keep getting into more and more trouble until he is banished. Which is where he is headed when Steele catches up with him."

Mac went to talk to Becky while Drew spoke to Cindy. She was conscious of them talking, just not what they were saying anymore. The talk of banishment was a scary thing to her.

Becky took her hand in her small one and told her about her day. "I've been going to dismal therapy today." She told her it was physical. "Yeah, that's what I said. Anyway, the woman helping me, the nurse that is hanging around until a better gig comes along, she told me, she said I was doing good and getting better every day."

Better gig? Mac wondered if the woman knew that she was teaching the child words that she'd repeat. Then she remembered Carlton and Hugh. The two of them tried to outdo each other when it came to old quotes or sayings.

"So I heard. The doctor sends me daily reports on your progress. They think you might be out of here next week if you keep this up." Becky looked at her mom then at her again. "She'll come with us too. Wherever you go, she'll be welcome as well. So long as you need her."

"My dad comes by to see me sometimes when Mommy goes to rest." Her voice was very low and she looked so frightened that Mac moved closer to her. "He said that I'm not a good girl and that I should suck you dry for what you did to him. You didn't hurt him, Mac, he did that all by his self. I seen him push the boat over and he let me get hurt. He's always doing stuff like that to me and Mommy."

So had the rest of them apparently. Her vest had shown that she did look at Adam when he approached the boat, and since hers had voice on it, they'd also heard what he'd said to her as he knocked the kayak away from the two rocks she'd wedged between. Had he just left them alone, both she and Becky would have gotten out of it with just a few minor cuts and bruises. As it was, he'd nearly killed them with his actions. The words he'd said to her were etched in her mind, and probably would be for a very long time, she thought.

"You fucking bitch, she's not worth saving. Give me this boat." He'd only meant, they'd surmised, to knock her free of the kayak and get in it himself. But the falls were too close and the current too strong for much more to happen than what did. She'd gone over, taking him with her as he held onto the kayak. His lack of a life vest had gotten him killed.

"Did you tell your mom that your dad was coming by and talking to you?" Becky said that she'd not. Her mom was afraid of her daddy too. "I can understand that, honey. But you need to have someone here with you when he's here. What I want you to do is to call for Aster. You remember her, don't you? The pretty young woman that comes to see you with your mom. Just call for her now and we'll make sure it works."

As soon as she said her name, Aster appeared in the room. She looked confused for a moment, but brightened when Mac explained to her what was going on. Of course, Aster then told her that she could call several of her friends and they'd come too. Billy and Donny were there in seconds, as was Connie, an elderly woman that she knew was Steele's grandmother.

"And you can always call for your mom too. You need to

let her know that your dad is coming by. She'll want to make sure that you're all right." Becky nodded and told her what she'd been up to. Explaining to the others there that she was going to be 'dopted soon.

"But I still have to work really hard too. Mom said that when I get to go to school, I need to be smart so that no one thinks I'm not trying. I'm going to try harder and harder every day." Mac wanted to hug Cindy and tell her what a great job she'd done in preparing her daughter for this huge change in her life. There would be problems, of that there was no doubt, but she was going to be all right too. She was already the smartest little girl she knew. And Mac was looking forward to having her in her life.

Just before the ghosts took their leave, stating that they had to rest up or return to work, each of them assured her and Drew that they'd be there when Becky needed them. It took a great deal off her mind to know that everyone wanted her as safe as she did. But when the room tightened not twenty minutes later, Mac knew that Adam had come to see them.

~~~

Cindy watched her husband with a great deal of fear. She also could feel hatred for the man who had tormented her most of her adult life, both in this life and the one she had now. And she knew as surely as she was standing there that he had killed her too when he'd tossed their daughter into the fast moving water, knowing that she could not swim. But Cindy was not going to let him hurt her little girl again, nor the people that were going to make sure that she grew up to be nothing like her mother. Becky would have a backbone. She'd be someone important; these people would make sure of that.

Stepping in front of the people in the room with Becky,

Cindy lifted her chin and glared at Adam when he started toward Mac. If today was going to be her last on this earth, she was going to make it count for something. He was going to know that she wasn't going to take his shit any more.

"What are you doing here? You told me that you didn't want to come here, not ever, even to see our daughter." Not actually what he'd said to her, but that was neither here nor there. He'd left them to their own, and as far as she was concerned, she was done with him too. Cindy told him to get out of there, to never return and bother any of them again. He of course told her to fuck off. His favorite line when things didn't go as he wanted.

"You think you can tell me what to do, bitch?" Adam laughed at her and she felt her anger at him manifest into a ball of fire in her belly. "You'll back off now, or so help me I'll make all those other times that I put you in your place look like a love tap. Besides, I'm not here to deal with your fucking ass. I want this woman here to jump from the window and rid the world of herself. Things are going on around here that just do not suit me. And if you think I'm letting you take my kid with you, then you're fucking—"

"You don't know the meaning of the word love, you overbearing bastard." It felt good to stand up to him, and she rubbed the hotness in her belly to feel the hatred she had. It gave her strength and courage that she'd never had before. And she loved it. "You'll back off this time, Adam, or so help me I'll do the hurting. I'm not your wife any longer, and I'm taking a stand right now."

No one moved, not even Adam, as the fire grew. When she pulled her hand away from her belly it was there…the flame was in her hand, and she knew that she could use it on him. Putting her hands out in front of her, Cindy felt empowered for the first time in her entire life when Adam backed up.

"You keep this up and I'll make sure you never go near that kid of ours again. See if I don't." The fire grew with every taunt he spewed at her; the heat of it was growing too. But while it burned, it didn't hurt. In fact, the more it grew the better she felt about herself. "I've had enough of you and this other bitch's shit for this lifetime. Don't make me have to deal with you too. Now you get over there and get rid of that fire. I'll deal with you in a bit. Damned uppity woman. I should have killed you a long time ago."

"You're going to deal with me right now, Adam. And then when I'm finished, there will be nothing left of you. Not even enough to be a spot on the floor." She had no idea if that was true, if what she was doing could hurt Adam, but she felt it could and moved closer to him only to have him backing away. "How does it feel to know fear, Adam? Do you like feeling like someone is going to hurt you? Do you—?"

"You're not going to hurt me. Now back the fuck off, Cindy, or so help me, you're going to regret it." Another step and he was nearly out of the room. It occurred to her that she was leaving them, the ones that were there to help her. But she knew this was right. The only way to do this. So that her daughter, her only child, would not see what she did to him. Standing up to the man that had lost her child for her was more important than anything she'd ever done before. "Get back, you fucking bitch."

The flame in her hand seemed to leap from her fingers to Adam. She realized then that it wasn't fire, but power. The heat of it was her anger and fear that had built up in her over the years. Letting more of her memories, her pain and her suffering, fill the ball in her hands, she saw it touch him again and again. Fingers of it reached out to where he had caused her pain on her body.

His face was burned when she remembered the time he'd slapped her hard enough to break her jaw. With the memory of the time he'd broken her arm over not having the right amount of change left over after buying groceries, his arm caught fire; she could see that the bones were broken too, in the same place hers had been. Every touch of the anger was a pain that she had suffered at his hands.

"Let it all go, you can do this." She knew the man standing close to her even though she'd never met him before in person. Steele Bennett was close enough to her that she could touch him. When she started to back away, lower her hands, he spoke again. "No. You need to finish this, Cindy. You need to stand up to him and finish what you started. He hurt you both, you and your daughter. Those memories, the ones where he hurt Becky, are the hottest of all."

Adam had knocked Becky out of her arms when she'd been two. She'd fallen from her arms to the floor and had been knocked unconscious. The doctors at the hospital had scolded her about being more careful in the future when she held her child, when all along she'd known that her husband had done it. The flame in her hands grew to be as tall as she was. And now it was white hot, blue flames dancing within it with reds and golds. But the white hot of her hatred for Adam was what gave it its power.

"You won't hurt anyone again." He was screaming, she realized. Crying, but still threatening her while he tried to beat the flames out. "Never again."

Shoving the heat at him, the flames of it took him. His entire body was engulfed in it, and he continued to scream and yell at her. As he started to disappear, his body becoming ash, so did her fear of him. As he became nothing, so he did

135

in her heart and mind. When Adam was gone, nothing left of him other than the few flakes of something on the floor, Cindy looked at Mr. Bennett, feeling her smile all over her body. She felt so good about what she'd been able to do for herself and for Becky.

"You knew that was what was going to happen?" He told her that he didn't. "Then why did you tell me to do it? What if he'd come at me?"

"Then I would have saved you. But you had it under control. You took care of the threat and vanquished it for all that he was making suffer and hurt. Including you and your child." She nodded, feeling pretty good about herself. "You will be safe now to stay with Becky until she doesn't need you anymore."

Cindy nodded and turned and looked at the door where her daughter was. The people in there, Mac and Drew, they'd take care of her better than she had ever been able to. Looking at Steele, she knew that she was finished here. He seemed to know that as well and smiled at her.

"I'd like to move on." He started to speak but she put up her hand. "No. I need to move on. My daughter is in good hands now. Better hands, really, and I don't need to be hanging around confusing her. Mac and Drew, they'll make sure that she'll be a good girl. Nothing like her parents. I need to move on anyway, while I'm feeling pretty good about myself."

"All right, but I think you're wrong about you and your daughter. She'll be a woman like her mother, like you. Strong and brave. Mac and Drew will be able to help her with that, support her, but what you did here today, that's what she'll remember most about you. How her mother stood up to a monster for her." Cindy started to deny that she was strong or brave, but Steele told her that she was. "Not many would have stood up to their abuser like you did. And you used your love for your daughter to defeat him. That is, in my opinion, the most powerful thing in the world. Especially when it comes from a mother."

"No, it was hate. I used my hate." Steele told her she was wrong. "I could see each time he hurt me. Every place he beat me. I thought of it and it happened to him."

"That was your love, Cindy. Your love that he threw back at you. The love that he scorned and ridiculed when you tried to give it to him. And you were able to use your love for your daughter to end that chain of meanness and hurt too. There is a difference between love and hate…a thin line, but there is. And I could see it. The moment you realized that you could save her, the power turned pure, white pure." He moved to her. "And you're probably right about moving on. You've done about all you can do for her now. Will you want to say good-bye?"

She thought about it. Really she did. And going in there to tell her that she was going to leave her now seemed harder than dealing with her husband. Looking back to where he'd disappeared, there was nothing left of him, not even a small mark to show that he'd ever been there. She wondered if she'd be that way, nothing to show that she'd ever been in this world. Nothing but the little girl in the other room, who she was sure would be a better person without her and Adam in her life.

"You will be remembered, Cindy." She looked at Steele when he spoke, almost as if he'd read her mind. "That little girl will remember what you've done for her long after she has children of her own. I promise you that. And when I tell Mac and Drew what you did, they'll make sure she knows and understands what you gave up to keep her safe. Becky will have you in her heart long after she is a memory too."

It felt...well, it felt wonderful to know that her little girl would be all right. There had been times in their life with Adam that she wondered if either of them would survive him. And even if only part of what Steele said was true, that her daughter would never forget her, Cindy knew that she was going to leave her in good hands. Better hands than hers.

"I'm ready." And she was too. Ready to meet the next phase of whatever this life had to give her. "Will you tell her that I loved her more than I did myself? That I will think of her often?"

"I will." As he brought his hands up and the light from his fingertips touched hers, Cindy moaned at how it felt touching her. Not the pain she had expected, but warmth, understanding, and compassion. As she faded away, watching the man who had done more for her in the last few minutes of her life here on earth than her husband or anyone else had done for her in all her years, she smiled at him and he smiled back. "Enjoy."

And she knew that she would. As her body became weightless she moved into the next room almost as if she were on a breeze. She saw her little girl then, being held by Mac as Steele told her what had happened. He made her sound as if she'd done something extraordinary, when all she had done was protect her family. As she watched, Becky turned to Drew and held his hand as she cried softly, and he in turn held the hand of the woman who would be the best mother of all to her child. Cindy felt better than she had ever felt in all her life.

"They will be fine." She looked over at the woman who spoke and sobbed when she saw her own mother. "You can see them if you wish...just once in a while, but you can see them. I came to see you often, and was so hurt that you didn't have a better life."

"I love you, Mom." Her mother told her that she loved her as well and put out her hand. "Is this what it's going to be like? You and I together?"

"Oh no, child." Cindy felt disappointment and her mom laughed. "Your father is there too. And Grandma. She's been fussing at us for days and days about you coming to see her. I told her you had good work to do and that you'd be along when you got it all done. I watched what you just did. And I've never been prouder of you than I was in that moment."

"I shouldn't have married him." Her mom, very practical, said that had she not, then there would have been no Becky. "That's right. I never thought of it that way before. She is going to be all right, isn't she, Mom?"

"Oh yes, honey, she'll be just fine. A little sad at times, and that's when you can go and comfort her. But she's strong, like you are. But I thank you for naming her for me. Proudest moment of my life—well, the second proudest—was when I was able to come back here and tell them what you'd done for me." Cindy asked her what the other moment was. "Why, when you were born and handed to me. Never seen a more beautiful baby in all my life. Your father nearly busted his buttons right off his shirt when he saw you. And then you had that little one and we danced around for days, telling everyone that would listen."

Laughing, she went with her mom as she told her what she was going to have from now on. It sounded too good to be true. Nothing to do all day but visit with the people who had left the world and gone to the other place. Be at peace and happy. Something that she was really looking forward to.

Cindy looked back over her shoulder, to the room where

her daughter was fading in the distance. She'd made the right choice in leaving her to grow up. And with the people who she was going to be with. Cindy knew that the others would do what they needed to make her a great woman. And her daughter would be too, with those strong people around her all the time. Then she saw her daddy and Cindy knew that she'd be all right as well.

CHAPTER 10

Drew tried not to move too quickly, but he needed to roll to his back. It was a stretching habit that he'd gotten into when he'd been home from the hospital long ago. If he stood or moved too quickly first thing after getting up, he'd be hurting all day. Then he felt the bed shift and nearly cried out when something heavy landed on his bare ass. This was not going to be good for him.

"Let me do this." Her voice was as dark as the room, her body warm as her hands moved up and down his spine then out over his shoulders and down. When he started to roll over, to tell her not to touch him on the scars, she told him to lay still for her. "I'm going to massage your muscles to get them warmed up. Then if you're a good boy, I'll let you fuck me."

"You'll *let* me fuck you? I never had any doubt that I would." She laughed as her hands moved gently up and down his spine again. It was painful, but not nearly as bad as it might have been if she was rougher. "Do you think this will work? I've never had anyone do this for me before."

"I should hope not. I'm as naked as you are, buster, and I don't even want to have to tell you what I'd do to you should someone even try." He felt his muscles begin to relax, the skin that was always so tight start to feel smoother, suppler. "Your skin isn't as bad as I thought it would be. I don't know why, but I expected it to be rough or something. The other time I saw it, you were mad at me and I didn't really look." He told her he was sorry about that, and she told him that she loved him very much.

"Skin grafts helped me a lot. I had to lay on my belly for weeks while they attached them to the skin that wasn't as badly damaged. Some took, some didn't. The fire wasn't as bad as it could have been." She asked him how long he'd been in the hospital. "Three months. It might have been shorter, but I had some trouble adjusting to some of the meds. It was difficult for me to take them; I didn't want to turn out like my mother. That was about the time that I decided I wasn't taking the pain pills. I think most of the doctors understood that and tried their best to work with me on it. A lot of the nurses had seen me come in when Mother hurt me badly enough that I'd end up on their floor. Of course, they all knew what happened this time to put me there." She wasn't sure, but Mac thought that he was too strong for that to have happened with the drugs. He had a willpower that astounded her. "Then I had to stay at a rehab center for a few more months. No one wanted to take me into their home as a foster child because of the injuries. Which I guess worked out well for me. I didn't have to worry about whether or not someone would hurt me again when I needed to have my bandages changed."

"That's too bad. They really missed out on getting to know a great kid, I bet." When he snorted at her, she laughed. "We can do this every day if it helps you. I love touching you and making your skin warm with my hands. And I have a hot tub coming too. The doctor said it would help my legs to have them worked out that way."

"My cock is hard as stone right now." She laughed and he

tried to roll over. "Let me feel you around me, Mac. I need to be buried deep inside of you."

As he rolled to his back, taking care not to hurt either of them, he looked up at Mac as she lowered herself over him. Holding his cock in his hand, he helped her as best he could until she was seated over him.

"I love how you fill me, Drew." He watched her face, the enjoyment that was there as she rode him, her hips moving back and forth. As she took her pleasure so did he, knowing that when she came he was going to take her hard. Her hands moved over her breasts, pulling and tugging at her nipples. Her body was firm and muscled, toned in ways that would make most body builders jealous. And it was all his, every single inch of her.

Reaching under her pillow where he knew her vibrator was, he turned it on low and slid it to her pussy. He knew the moment she felt when it touched her clit. Her gait was stronger then, her pussy tightened around him twice as she moaned and said his name.

"Come for me, baby. Let me see you when you do." She shook her head, telling him that she wanted this to last. Touching the vibrator firmly against her, she nearly bucked off him as she took his hand in hers. "Come, Mac. Come now."

She bowed back nearly in half as she came. Her hands were so tight on her nipples that he wondered if she'd hurt later. When she screamed out his name, telling him she was coming again, he sat up, pulled her body to his, and suckled hard on just the tip of her nipple as she held him to her. Cupping her ass tighter to his groin, he rolled them over as her feet wrapped around him and he settled between her thighs. His cock so full, his balls so painful, that he knew a single movement would have him emptying into her immediately.

"Christ, I love you." Drew pounded her hard, leaving no room for her to catch her breath as she came twice more before he felt his own climax tighten his balls to his body. "Come for me, Mac. Come with me."

Her nails dug deep into his shoulder, her heels into his thighs. As she came, her body bowing up off the bed as she cried out, his cock exploded his own release inside of her as his balls filled again. Dizzy with the need to come again, needing to feel her as she tightened her pussy around him, milking him, Drew didn't stop. When he came the second time, his entire body feeling the release, he knew that he was going to die from pleasure as surely as he knew he was in love with her.

The room was bright with light when he woke the next time. He stood up slowly, marveling at how well he felt when he made his way to the bathroom. The phone was ringing when he walked by it and figured it wasn't for him so he ignored it. Drew stepped under the hot spray and washed the rest of his sleep from his body. He was feeling pretty good when he was pulling on his clothing twenty minutes later.

Drew knew that Mac was an early riser and as he walked by the window, he could see her in the yard with Rory. They were playing fetch, the dog's favorite game. The dog had not let either of them out of his sight since they'd gotten home from the hospital yesterday after seeing Becky. It was fine by him. Rory had been like an early warning system for the neighbor they'd been avoiding.

After making the bed and going down to the lower level, he wasn't really surprised to see Kari and little Aster there in the kitchen. Everyone was leaving tomorrow right after the small wedding tonight, but she and Steele had decided to stay with them and he was glad for it. They were going to stick around and help with his mom. Dealing with her wasn't going to be easy, he thought. Not like it had been with Adam. He was going to have to do this himself. There wasn't anyone to do it for him. And he really wasn't sure that he wanted them to.

"Mac said to tell you that she was going into town today." Drew asked Kari what was going on as Mac came into the house. She looked spitting mad and he watched her carefully as she tried to curb her language around the baby.

"That fu...that bad woman just approached me about selling my fu...my darned house again. Why doesn't she mind her own da...darned business?" Kari laughed as she pulled Aster out of the high chair that had been brought with them, and was still laughing as she left the room. "What the hell is so funny now?"

"You. And I'd really like to know what sort of conversation that darned woman had with you that got you all ticked off." Mac said she hated him. Drew pulled her into his arms and held her as she laughed too. "What did she want, really? Anything I can do to fix it for you?"

"She wants my house and property. Now she's saying that we're running a hotel here with all these people coming and going all the time. I pointed out to her that she's not going to run one here either if I have anything to do about it." Mac laughed again. "I thought she was going to swallow her tongue when I told her I knew about her little plan to run my business and take the property of all the other people along this side of the river. Did she think that she was the only one that knew anything? Don't answer that. I know that she does."

"Oh, that reminds me, Roger called and left a message. I didn't pick up when it rang, I was looking for you." She said he'd called her on her cell phone when she'd been in the yard.

145

"Everything all right?"

"Yes. I guess." She sat down in the chair next to his. "Apparently we now own the land that Becky's parents had. Steele figured out a way to make it so that Becky would get it when she turns eighteen, but until then, we own it to use as we see fit. What does that mean, as we see fit?"

He had no idea what that meant, but said that he'd ask if she didn't. There was more, he could see it on her face. Getting up, letting her work through it, he pulled out the cereal that they both preferred for breakfast, as well as two bowls and the milk. Silverware was already on the table in a crockery container, so when she handed him a napkin, he knew she was ready and asked her about what was bothering her.

"Your mom. She was out there this morning when I took Rory out." He wondered if she'd said anything to her. "No. She just watches us. Rory has learned to ignore her as well. Do you suppose she's waiting for us to leave to she can pounce on us? Nothing that goes on with these people would surprise me anymore. I mean, they're not nice people, are they?"

"Most are, really, but we hit the jackpot when it comes to evil spirits, I think. I'm going to talk to her today. Kari said you were going into town. If you don't mind, I'll do it while you're gone." She nodded as she ate her breakfast. "You did remember that we're getting hitched today, didn't you?"

"Yes. I'm excited for that. Are you sure you want to do this today? And not wait for a few days?" He told her that it was wrong to have them all waiting around and he wanted to get it over with. Her grin told him that she was planning something big. "Anyway, yes. Go ahead and do what you can about her. I know that it's going to be rough on you, but you'll get through it all right."

"Steele is going to be here in the event something goes

wrong." And he knew that plenty could go wrong. Even with the story that he'd told them about Cindy and her dealing with her husband, he knew that things could have gone really bad for all of them. "You have fun."

As soon as Mac, Dillon, Addie, and Kari left, having decided it would be a fun way to get to know each other, Drew went to find Steele and the others. It was time to get this finished. And if she had to be banished, which he was betting she would, he was glad that it was going to be dealt with as well. Drew wanted to get on with his life now that he had a family and a wife.

"You ready for this?" Nick was standing next to him as they made their way out to the yard that his mother had been hanging out in. As soon as she saw him, she started telling him what he was going to do and that she was going to make him pay. For the most part he ignored her in favor of the man in front of him. "You do know that Steele or I can just deal with it and you won't have to be involved."

"I know that. But I have to see why, if she even has a reason, she's still around. And why she wants to hurt Mac. I know that she's never loved me, and I guess that's fine now, but what did Mac ever do to her?" Nick said he didn't know, but in his opinion most people did things simply because they could. "Plus, I need to see if she can tell me why she hated me so much."

"She might not have a reason for that either. It might just be who she is." He'd thought of that too, so he didn't say anything. Drew really wasn't sure if her reason was going to give him peace either, but he knew it was time. "We're here for you, any way you want to handle it."

"I know that."

He also had discovered something else when they all

came to help him. He really loved these men and their wives. Drew knew that in the coming months it was going to be hard for them without him there. They were running short on staff now as it was. But he just couldn't do it anymore. It was high time he got out while he still had his sanity. If he'd ever had any.

His mother was standing on the very edge of the property, just waiting, as if she knew that he'd come to her. And if her looks were any indication, she was not happy with him. Nor the rest of them. Steele sat on the lawn furniture that had been left out on the property and the rest of them took the table. They were set, it seemed.

~~~

"Mother." Belinda wanted to go over there and slap that smirk right off her boy's face, but she knew that for whatever reason, she wouldn't be able to get that close to him. Not just because of the wall that was keeping her where she was on this side of the yard, but the men with him as well. "I've come here to find out what you want from me and my wife."

"Wife? You're not married. And you won't ever be either. You need to get somewhere I can sit down with you and talk. I don't know what you're doing with these people, but this is going to stop right now." He only stared at her and Belinda felt her anger move over her body like a hot shower. "Did you hear me? I said you're not going to hanging around here any longer. Let's you and I go and find a place to stay, and I'll try my best to not hurt you too much. And don't you dare act like you have no idea what your beating will be for either. You've been acting out for some time now."

"No. You're not going to hurt me ever again. And if things go the way I want them to, you won't be coming around either." She started to draw back her hand and show him just how bad she was going to hurt him when he spoke again. "Did you know that you're dead, Mother?"

Something touched her mind. Fire. Screaming. But before it could take a place in her head and let her see what that was about, Drew told her that she'd been dead for more than seventeen years.

Pain ran up her body. Her arms were burning. So were her legs. Even as it touched her face, she knew that he was telling the truth. Pain screamed over her. She had been on fire. Her clothing was melting against her skin in a way that no matter what she did to try and put it out, all it did was burn hotter. She was melting, like the witch in that movie that used to scare her boy. And she knew that no amount of water was going to put her out. But instead of telling him he was right, Belinda lashed out at the boy.

"Shut up. What kind of fool do you take me for? I'm no more dead than you are." But the feeling in her head wasn't going away. "I'm not going to tell you again that I want you to come along with me, Andrew. I've been waiting here long enough for you to come out of that whore's house."

"Don't call her that again. She's my wife. Has it occurred to you why you're never hungry, Mother? Why you can walk through things rather than around them? And why do you think you can't come in and talk to us? I'm sure that you've tried to cross the barrier. Did you not think there was a reason for it?" She had worked on that, several times, and still had no answer. But she didn't like the fact that he was embarrassing her in front of these strangers, and told him so. "These are my friends. My family, if you will. Better than you ever were to me. These men have done more for me in the last several days than you did in my entire lifetime. Living with you was a nightmare since the first day I can remember."

"You think living with you was fun? Christ, boy, you were the dumbest person I ever met. And you thought that anything I did for you wasn't good enough." He asked her what she'd thought she'd done for him. "I didn't abort you, did I? I didn't sell you when I was so broke that I couldn't get a fix, did I? And let me tell you, I had plenty of offers too. Even when I should have had one of them doctors suck you out of me when you were just nothing more than a dot on the page, I knew that I'd hate you with all that I was."

That shut him up. Or she thought it had until she realized he was laughing at her. She was pretty sure that she'd not said a word that was funny, so he had to be laughing at her. Looking down at her clothing, she wondered if she'd gotten something on her. There was a burnt mark on her dress and when she rubbed at it, two more came up.

"You want to know how you died, Mother?" That tone again. She remembered that tone he had when he was telling her something she didn't know. Which had been plenty, but she never let him get away with it. "You tried to kill me by setting fire to me when I was tied to the posts in the house that I had torn down."

Screams again. Heat and blurry images had her taking a step back. She was afraid that something was coming for her. The bright fire burning around her had her crying. But when she looked at Andrew to tell him to help her, she could see the little boy he'd been, tied to the posts she'd made out of pipe.

Bits and pieces were coming back to her. No, that wasn't it, they were slamming into her like a swatter on a fly. It had been his birthday and he wanted pizza. She'd knocked him around until he fell back.

"You were bothering me about your pizza. I told you that you no more deserved it than I did a good fuck." Belinda put her hands on her head when the buzzing started again. "I want you to come home with me, Andrew. I've had enough of your shit for one day. I don't feel so good. I need for you to score me a good one."

"You're dead." She told him to shut up. "You set fire to me with a can of lighter fluid then lit a match. I guess you didn't think it was hot enough because you sprayed me again and the flame went back to you. It caught the gown you had on first. Then, because of the amount of alcohol you had in your system, I can only assume that you were like a candle wick and it burned you from the inside out. I watched you. I was in so much pain that I couldn't move from what you'd done to me, so I watched you die in front of me."

"You did it to me." He told her that it wasn't possible for him to have done anything to her as he'd been tied up and hurt too. "No. You tried to kill me by pestering me to death with your constant whining. I remember that part. And I'm not dead. I'm as alive as you are. Or you are for now. I'm going to kill you like I should have long ago. You're nothing but a liar."

But that wasn't true either. She had a feeling that what he was saying was at least partly true. There had been a fire. She could see it now. But it had not killed her. She'd been...there was no way she was dead. She was as alive as he was.

"You're dead, ain't you? You done went and killed yourself when you saw what a mess you were gonna be." He shook his head and put out his hand to her. "What do you think I am, stupid? You're going to put cuffs on me and have them welfare people take my money from me. That card was the only reason you never got smothered to death in your crib. Those people came around so much, I felt like I should have charged rent to them."

His hand sort of froze right there. She wondered briefly if she could have slapped it, but was genuinely afraid to try. There was something different about her boy, and she didn't like it. Looking at the other men with him, she knew there was something different about them, something unlike the other men that she knew. And while she didn't know what it was, she was afraid of them. More than she wanted to admit right now.

"Why did you keep me when there were so many others out there that might have treated me better? Kept me warm in the winter, or even made sure I had food all the time?" She snorted at him. "Why, Mother? Why did you even have me if I was never going to be anything to you but more money?"

"Why do you think you deserved any better than what I deemed you were fit for? Hmm? Did you have to have it better than me? I'm guessing you think you did. There doesn't have to be any other reason than that, don't you think? I mean, I was getting some money from the government assistance people before you came along. Then that lady came by the day after you were born...I was actually thinking of smothering you if I remember correctly, but she said I could have a bunch more shit if I kept you. Even got a cell phone out of the deal. Then as the checks came in, so did my need for you to be around. It's why I never sold you when I could have. I liked having the stuff that came with shitting you out of me. And it's not like I let you starve, did I? I mean, I made sure you had something." She looked at the man on the chair and shrugged at him. "He makes it sound like I never did shit for him. I think not killing him every day should make me a saint, not made out to be some kind of monster like he is. Damn it, he owes me for not killing him."

"No, I'm betting you did plenty for him." She started to

152

smile at the man, liking him all of a sudden. But he spoke up before she could tell him more. "The money that was to go for his care, did you spend it on him or the next fix? And the time you left him in his bed with three bottles of watered down formula so you could go out that night and party. Was that for his benefit as well? You left him for three days, didn't you? Or how about the time you sent him into the store to steal some food for your fuck buddy? And let him stay in jail for a week before you remembered to go and get him? I think the reason you did go get him was that you needed him to go out and steal again. Isn't that right, Belinda?"

"How the fuck do you know all that?" He told her that there was little that he didn't know about her since she'd died. "I'm not dead, I'm telling you. Stop fucking saying that. I'm not dead, and I refuse to listen to you saying that again like you know better. Just shut the fuck up about that."

But the man stood up and walked to her. When he moved through her, just walked right through her, she felt sick; her body even felt like he'd dipped her in something dirty. When she turned to tell him to fuck off, she saw a woman standing behind them that she'd seen before. The woman from the hospital. The welfare woman. She didn't look any better than Belinda felt. Like someone had beat her to shit and left her in the road to be run over a few times.

"I lost my life because of you." The woman came toward her, her body looking more like she'd been rotting for some time the closer she got to her. "And when I tried to explain to them that you'd be a good mother, it only took me one look into the house when you'd left your baby there to know what a terrible mistake I'd made. Leaving your house cost me my life. I was raped and killed even as I tried to go to the office and report you. Then they dropped me into a dumpster, just left me there for no one to find. Now, because of you, I'm in a landfill where my family will never find me."

"You're dead? Well, it serves you right for thinking you might know more about shit than I did. And so you know, I never asked you for that money or the phone. You came right in my room and gave it to me like you wanted me to have it. Back off, girl, before I have to hurt you." As she got closer to her, Belinda felt the burning again. This time it was all over her, and as she looked down at her clothing, she could see the flames eating away at her gown. And beating at it only made it worse. "Make it stop, Andrew. Make this stop."

"I can't. And even if I wanted to, I wouldn't. You made your bed, now you have to lie in it."

It was getting harder and harder to breathe. And as she tried her best to put out the flames, she saw her son, and he was on fire too…not the man before her, but the kid from before.

He had been wanting a pizza, a hot one for his birthday. She remembered that now. He'd been driving her crazy all week about it. Telling her to save her money because that's what he wanted. No kid of hers was going to tell her what to do.

Taking the broom handle to him, she'd knocked him out. And while he was down for the count, Belinda had tied him to her posts as she'd done many times before. But this time he didn't scream like she wanted him to. Didn't beg her to let him down. And that pissed her off.

"Would it have made any difference for you to have just shut the fuck up and left me alone? Let me live out my life without it coming to this, Mother? This was all your fault." It was getting harder to see him, the heat was making her sick to her stomach. And as the flames tore at her, burned into her, she could see her son rolling on the floor to put his own fire out. When she'd dropped to her knees to do the same, she'd got caught up in her new rug she'd traded for sex and it wrapped around her like a melting blanket.

"It hurts. Make it stop."

The fire burned on as she watched the men move away. Her son, the fucking boy from hell, was leaving her to hurt. As she reached out to touch him, to drag him down with her, he turned and put up his hands. This heat was a different kind and it knocked her back. It was white hot and her body started to come apart with it. Looking at her son, Belinda had a sudden thought.

She was going to hell for sure. And it was all his fault.

CHAPTER 11

Mac had spoken to all the men. When she'd not been able to talk to Drew after they'd gotten home today, she reached out to the others to see if he was all right. Steele assured her that he was doing well, but was a little wiped out. Hugh told her that he was getting dressed and that he would talk to her in a little while. At the time that seemed a little strange that he was getting ready so early. But then Aster had come to talk to her with Carlton and Billy.

"This can't be good." Billy told her everything was fine but Aster said nothing. Carlton, in his old world ways, told her that some things were harder to get into your head than they were your heart. "You're saying that his mother hurt him."

"She did. That woman surely did. But he's a better man for it, I think. Much better than I think I might have been should it have been me." Carlton made her want to get a hug from him, something she knew was impossible. "You're going to be fine, my dear. Very fine now that that evilness is taken care of.

Aster nodded at the chair and Mac so badly wanted to tell her no, she needed to stand. But Aster seemed to understand that and said nothing. The two men nodded when she was sure it was clear she wasn't going to fall apart, and left them after a few minutes. Mac looked at Aster as she spoke.

"She hurt him in her honesty. It was more than likely the first time she'd been that way to him since he'd been born." Aster moved through the room, not taking care as she usually did not to walk through the furniture rather than around it. "Some people don't deserve to have someone that loves them. And he did. All the way up until he banished her. He did it himself, which I have to say surprised me a little."

"Belinda told him that she hated him, didn't she?" Aster said that she had. "I knew that she did. I mean, there is no way that she could have ever loved him and done the things that she did. He's such a wonderful and loving man. I wonder how she ever lived with herself in the way she treated him. I love him so much. Is he all right?"

"He will be in a few hours. Once you come down the stairs to him." Mac sat down then. She was weak with her pain for Drew. "Did you know that she'd been planning his death for a long time? She told him that she'd planned to smother him in his crib at the hospital until she found out that she'd get paid for keeping him. Then it sort of became a game for her, I think. Thinking of ways to make him pay for her keeping him alive."

"It figures. I'm betting that he wasn't her first pregnancy either. That other children were killed by her. I can see where she would think that it was a good idea to rid herself of unwanted pregnancies. But to be honest with you, I think Drew knew that she might have wanted him dead, don't you?" Aster only smiled. "He's going to be all right now. I'm going to make sure of it. We're going to have a long and very happy life together."

"You will. Of that I have no doubt." Mac leaned back and waited for whatever else Aster had to say to come out. She really liked the woman and knew that had she lived, they would have been good friends. "He won't go back to working with my brother. I don't think he was cut out for it, and Steele agrees. Drew is very tenderhearted and he has been abused long enough. He, in my opinion, needs to be free of things like that. Besides, I think he's going to be perfect at his next job."

"Drew said he'd help them out when they needed it." Aster said that he wasn't going to be called on no matter what. "They're cutting him out then? I'm not sure he's going to like that any better than he did working the job. Do you?"

"Yes, he'll love it. But they're giving the two of you just what you need. Peace and quiet and a chance to live out your days free of what neither of you bargained for. There will be a time when they call on you, but it will not be for helping with their clients." Mac asked her what she meant. "For the children left behind. They'll ask you to help with them. And I'd very much like for you to consider doing it for us. For the children."

"I don't understand. You mean the children of the people that are ghosts? You want us to take them on? You can't be serious. We know nothing about what sort of issues and problems that these kids will have. Hell, I don't even know what sort of issues Becky will have. I don't think we can do that." Aster told her that they were perfect for the job because they had more insight on the pains of growing up than any one she knew. "And you think we can handle that? I'm not sure about that, Aster. Taking on Becky is sort of scary for us. Neither of us have a lot of experience with people, much less children. And I'm thinking these kids will need a great deal more than we have for them. Both emotionally and physically."

"You have plenty of both, Mac. They won't come to you

as Becky has, however. These children will need a guiding hand in what they are left to deal with. All of them will have scars, deep ones, but most of those no one will see but you and Drew. Those scars will be what you help them with." She asked her how. "The same way you have dealt with the death of your father. The way you worked through your grief when others thought you'd fail."

Mac started to tell her that she'd not had any trouble dealing with her father's death when the younger woman shook her head. She had…Mac knew that she'd had some issues, but not many. Working hard at being independent wasn't a problem…not really, was it?

"I devoted myself to my job. I don't think that will help us at all when we work with these kids." But it had helped her and she was pretty sure that Aster knew that as well. Several weeks after her father's death, Mac had ended up in the hospital from exhaustion. And when she'd gotten out, she'd never slowed. But it had gotten her through it all. Working hard had been her therapy.

"These children, they'll need the same from you. Your ability to see where they need help and also the knowledge that they need their space. Work them hard, show them some things, and you'll all come out on top. But most importantly, show them that you love them with all that you are." Aster smiled at her as she continued. "One or two of them might even surprise the world at what you will be able to give them."

Mac didn't ask her how she knew what was going to happen. Nor did she ask her what sort of things these children might have gone through that they'd need her and Drew. To her, the two of them had enough issues to fill several books, but Aster only sat there. Then it occurred to her what she wanted them to do.

160

"You want us to open our home to a bunch of wayward kids. Try and get them back on track from the tragedy that has come to them." Aster only smiled. "You know, I thought I liked you, but I'm beginning to think you're a sadist. I don't know shit about wayward kids any more than I do getting them on the right path. Wherever the hell that might be. And where do you think I'm going to house them? I have a four bedroom house, which two of the rooms are now occupied."

"You'll be fine. And there will be plenty of funds to help you with the new buildings too." Before Mac could ask her about the new buildings and funds, Aster stood up. "I must go now. The wedding starts soon and I have to go and see Drew. He really is all right, Mac. In fact, I'm thinking he's never been better than he is right at this moment. And all thanks to you."

"I love him. But don't think this is going to get you off the hook, young lady. I want answers, not more half statements." Aster smiled and said that he loved her as well. "This thing you have going on in your head, is it a done deal? I mean, what if we don't want to do it?"

"Oh, you have to do it now. Didn't I mention that? Oh well. The first kid is right at your doorstep as we speak. He needs more than just a home to live in, but love as well." With that she disappeared and Mac heard the doorbell ringing at the bottom of the stairs. She was going to…well, she was going to get back at the woman if it was the last thing she did.

Mac didn't even bother going to see who it was. There were enough people in the house now, living and dead, to help them deal with it until after she was married. Getting up to go to the bathroom, she wondered what sort of things Aster was telling Drew, and hoped he got more information. They were going to be so screwed if they thought she was going to be a motherly type to these kids.

The women of the men she'd come to admire helped her finish getting dressed. Vinnie was there as well with her grandmother, and they took her aside to tell her about young James. He was the young man that had come to the wedding uninvited and hungry.

"He's lost. I don't mean like he had no idea where he lived, but his mind is a jumble of thoughts and issues that no fifteen year old should have to think on. In his short lifetime, he's had some very terrible things happen to him. And so you know, he's going to need a lot of things to help him out, clothing and such. He only has the things he has on." Mac asked Vinnie what sort of things had happened to him and why he wasn't at his home. "Family issues. On a grand scale, I'm afraid. His stepfather can't hold down a job, and when he does have one, it's not a very well-paying job and he's sort of terrible with money. James's mother is lazy and not at all very loving. Her idea of a hug is…well, the younger children get much more of her time than James ever had. You see, we think it's because James isn't her husband's boy and James gets slighted a lot. So they made up this nonsense about how he needed to eat less when there wasn't enough food to feed the man's own child. I'm afraid that he's gone to the other extreme on that now. Too thin for a boy his size. James has been…well, he's been out on his own longer than need be. And now he can't go home either."

"Why not?" Vinnie looked at her grandmother then back at her without answering her. "Why can't he go home now? Did he do something that is so horrible that I don't want to know?"

"Oh no. He's a good boy. Polite and sweet. The stepfather has told him that he is not to return because they don't love him, that he is undeserving of any kind of love. Can you imagine someone saying that to a child? That he wasn't deserving of love? They also told him that he isn't loveable and that he will never be so. I believe them to be the worst kind of parents." Mac said that that couldn't be true and asked what his mother had said. "Nothing. I think she feels that her life is all sewn up now with this man in her life, and her son is going to mess it up for her and the other boy, James's half-brother. As I said, she is lazy and has his child to care for. She said that he is to leave her property and never to return. When he did as he was told, she said that he abandoned them and he wasn't to return to them. The stepchild and the one she has by her husband is enough for them, she told him."

Christ, where the fuck did these people come from? "Tell someone to set him up in the bedroom on the lower floor. After we're married, Drew and I will figure out something to help him." Vinnie nodded and smiled. "You tell me that he has some sort of magical power right now and I might chance hitting you. I have had enough thrown at me today...for a lifetime, I think."

"No, he's human. But you should know that Drew said the same, that you would help him after the ceremony. I think the two of you are going to be perfect for this job." Mac wasn't so sure and said as much. "No, you'll do fine at this, and these children will bask in your love for them. And you will have a very long time to help a lot of people. And I'll help."

Mac wasn't sure that Vinnie meant she was going to help with the kids or help in bringing her more. Either way, she was too busy now to think about it much. As soon as the music started, she stood in line as the other women made their way down the stairs. For a quick wedding, the house had been decorated by professionals and there were so many flowers in the large living room that Mac wondered if the florist in town had been the only place they'd called. Not to mention there had to be over two hundred guests in her house. Too many to consider this thing small by any means.

Mac was seriously thinking that she was going to murder them all before this was over. But they'd just come back as ghosts and be more of a pain in her ass. Smiling, she made her way to the man she loved.

By the time they said they loved each other and the clergyman pronounced them man and wife, Mac was too worried about the boy to stand in line for the reception. Going to the room where he'd been put, she wasn't surprised to find that Drew had come with her. They were in this together, it seemed. As soon as she knocked on the door and was bid entrance, Mac knew that they were doing the right thing for him. The kid looked as lost as she felt.

"Hello, James. Welcome to the family. I'm Mac and this is Drew." He told her his full name then flushed brightly. "You are going to be safe here. I want you to know that right now. Safe and happy."

~~~

Drew watched his new wife fuss over James. He'd been beaten up recently and his clothing was torn up and dirty. As she had him go and find him something to wear, Mac was telling James where the shower was and got him some clean towels. When he returned with a pair of his jogging pants and a tee shirt that had been in some of Mac's things, he found her sitting on the edge of the bed crying. The bathroom door was closed and he could hear the shower running.

"What is it, love? Did he hurt you?" She shook her head and told him he was hurt, and she wasn't sure how to help him. "We can bandage him up pretty good. I saw that you have a nice kit in the kitchen. I'll go and get it."

"No, that's not it. But he will need you to help him with a couple of cuts. No, I mean that he's hurt by all this. And ashamed. Who does that to their own child?" He had no answer for her and held her while she cried. As soon as the water turned off, Mac stood up and said she'd make sure that everyone knew that there was going to be one more for dinner. "And they'd better be nice to him too. I'm about ready to toss them all out on their asses for putting this on us on our wedding day."

"They will." As she left him with James, he wondered again what the hell they were going to do for these kids. As soon as James came out of the bathroom with a towel around his too thin body, Drew knew that come hell or high water, they'd make it work. "I have some clothing for you. Tomorrow we'll go into town and get you things that will fit."

"You don't have to do that, sir. I'll be able to wear my stuff if I can get a way to wash it up. I don't want to cause you any trouble." Drew just handed him the clothing. As the kid dressed, Drew took an inventory of the cuts and bruises on his body. Most of them were superficial, but they'd need to be cleaned. And Drew was glad to see that none of them were life-threatening. When he was dressed, Drew asked him to have a seat.

"We're going to help you out, James, starting now. You'll stay here for a long as you want. No, that's not right. You'll stay here until we say otherwise. Neither my wife nor I want you to be out on your own again." The boy looked skeptical, and that was all right for now. "You'll live here and go to school too. Follow the rules we give you. You should know as of right now that I'm not sure what they'll be, only that we want you to trust us that you're going to be safe here."

"I thought that before." It slipped out of his mouth, Drew

165

knew, before he could think he might have kept his mouth shut. When he said he was sorry, Drew told him that he had to be honest if he wanted his help. "I don't know what do to either."

"That much we have in common." When he heard his belly growl, Drew knew that was something that he could take care of right now. "There is a lot of food in the other room. I want you to eat a little. Not because I don't want you to have it, but I'm betting it's been a while since you've had a real meal, right?"

"Yes, sir. I've been out on my own for about three months. I didn't like stealing, but there were times when I didn't have any choice in the matter." He moved to his torn clothing and took out a beaten little notebook. "I've been keeping track of what I had to take. I'm ashamed to show you this, if you want to know the truth, and you might just kick me out again after you see it. But I plan to pay them back. Every penny of it."

"And you will too. Starting Monday you'll work for us. I know that my wife has some boats that need to be repaired before summer, and there are any number of things that have to be done around the business and house. All right?" James said nothing but nodded. "You'll save half the money we pay you after you pay off some of your debt, and the rest is yours to do with what you want."

"You're going to pay me?" Drew gave him a price, not having any idea if it was even close to minimum wage. "You gonna take some of it for room and board too?"

"No. As of the moment you walked through our doors you became family, and we don't charge for family to live here. You'll help us out, do the dishes or take out the trash, but not pay rent. One of the rules I just thought of is, if you have homework, that comes before everything else. You'll need a good education, and that's the best way to start." The boy looked skeptical and really, Drew didn't blame him. "For now I want you to rest, relax, and get to know the others here. They're family too, and will help you if you need them."

As the two of them made their way to the living room where the others were, Hugh came up to James and welcomed him to the family, and handed him a plate of cheese and crackers. Pieces of fruit were on the plate as well. Everyone, it seemed, was going to make sure this kid was all right. As James was introduced to everyone, Drew watched him eat slowly. He wanted it all, they could tell, but eating slowly kept him from getting sick. After about twenty minutes it was as if they'd known James his entire life and he was just another member of the extended family.

Drew went to find Mac. She was standing in the living room watching James as he worked the room.

"We'll have to tell him a few things. Like the fact that he's talking to a vampire and a cat right now, and that most of us see ghosts all the time." Drew laughed and Mac did as well. "We'll be able to keep him safe, won't we, Drew? I mean, we can do this, don't you think? I hate the fact that he's alone and that his mother.... She needs her ass kicked."

"I agree with you on that one. But I think he's going to be all right as well. But he does need to have some clothing and things of his own. His room is set up…Vinnie and Alexandra saw to that while I made a few calls. I want him to see a doctor, just to make sure he doesn't have any broken bones or such." She said that she would take him into town in the morning. "I think he'd do better with me taking him. Man to man, you know."

He watched her as she nodded while keeping an eye on James. He was moving around the room, talking to those that spoke to him, but for the most part he was keeping to himself. And he kept a constant eye on the front doors. It occurred to Drew he was waiting for someone to come and get him. Or the police to be called. Drew wanted this kid to feel safe here, and he was determined to make it happen.

As the party began to wind down, Alexandra came to talk to him and Mac. The first thing she said was that she was sorry. Next she told them what she'd done regarding James.

"I have gone to get him some things that he can wear. I have some connections with some shop owners, and they were all too willing to give him a hand up in this." When Mac said that they were going to pay her back, Alexandra waved her off. "You are going to need help on occasion, and it's my turn to help you. We all want this to work. There are too many children out there that are more lost than this child is, and we want them as safe as you do. A few items from a store that I own is not going to break me. Oh, and I might have gotten him a few things for school as well."

Drew said nothing. It wouldn't have mattered, and he was a little relieved that some of the work had been done for him. It was a daunting task to think about taking a young man to a mall when he'd been down on his luck for so long. Mac asked her what she knew about his parents.

"His father, his biological father, is not in the picture. And before I forget, I've contacted a friend of mine and had the little support he was sending to James's mother stopped. It'll now be put into a bank account for the boy's education until you two decide what you need done with it. I'm assuming that you have no real need for his support, but it's taken care of. I don't believe they used it on him anyway, so there is no reason they should continue to get support for someone they barely supported in the first place anyway." Drew thought it was a good idea and so did Mac. "His stepfather is a bastard. Not in the birth sort of way, but just in general. He works when it suits him. And when he has no job, he sits about the house lamenting about how the world or government, whichever he has trouble with on any particular day, treats him badly, and that he can never catch a break. I would very much like to break him in a few places."

"Don't." Alexandra cocked a brow at him. He thought of all the things she could do to him in that second, millions of things flittered through his head, but he had a point to make. "Please don't break any part of him. He has other children to care for even if he does a piss poor job of it. I don't want to take in the rest of them, thanks."

"Good point. But the mother…there's a piece of work if I ever saw one. Beyond lazy. She has no education to speak of other than a freshman high school term that she didn't even finish when she got pregnant with the boy. Her idea of good parental skills is to bully them more than most children would, sit upon her ample bottom, and complain with her husband how the world treats her when she'd tries so hard. The only thing she's tried hard at in her married life is to make herself look like a slob and not care for the one person in her life that loved her despite what she'd done to him." Drew asked her if there was anyone else that might come for James. "No. He has grandparents that are devastated that their daughter did this to him, and they've been trying for weeks to find him. I don't think they'll contest you taking the child in so long as they can see him when they want. They're good people, so you don't have to worry about him with them. He loves them as well."

"Then why didn't they…?" Mac looked at him before she finished the sentence. "They can't take him in or they cannot see the other children, right?"

"I would say so. This young man, he's going to need a man in his life, as well as someone like you, Mac. Loving and hard at the same time. You'll both be the best thing for him. Now and in the future. I'm so glad that we found you when we did. And I'm sure that James is as well." Drew looked over at the boy and wondered what he was thinking. He was sure it was the same thoughts that had gone through his head when he'd been a kid and his mother had done some of the things she'd done to him. "Drew, he's never known a man to hug him other than his grandfather. A loving touch, nor one that was done with a less than harsh hand. He'll be terrified at first, but if you love him, like I know you will, he'll give you more than any other person in the world can give you."

By the time everyone left them, Drew realized that he was going to be a father. In a roundabout sort of way, he supposed, but a dad all the same. None of them would be of his blood, more than likely none of them would call him dad either. But he knew, deep in his heart, that he was going to be better than most biological fathers were, and he'd make sure that his kids knew he loved them. Kissing Mac on the nose, he made his way to the deck to find his boy and help him navigate his way in this stupid world.

James was asleep on the lounge chair, a half-eaten sandwich on the plate that was resting on his belly. His shoes were worn, and Drew had a feeling that they were too small as well. He knew how quickly a kid could grow by just watching little Aster at six months. Instead of waking him, not sure of the reception he'd get, Drew sat down and looked out over the river that ran lazily behind their house.

It was a give and take thing, the water that looked so calm most of the time. He knew that just up from where he sat the water rushed over the falls in such a way that it destroyed more than most people could realize. Trees bent their large bodies over it where he could see, some even dipping into its chilling depths for whatever reason. There were creatures there too, both in and surrounding it, that depended on it for not just water, but food sources as well. Flowers would take over the banks in the spring and summer. In the fall, as the weather was now, there would be leaves falling on it to make a slow and most time traitorous way to the larger rivers that it fed. All in all, he thought, it was the most perfect eco system he knew.

The chair creaking behind him had him smile. James was awake finally. Not that there was anything pressing he wanted to talk to him about, but he did want to spend some time with him. Drew was looking forward to watching him grow and mature into a man.

"Thank you." Drew looked over at James when he spoke. "You don't have to keep me here, but I do want to thank you for what you've done for me so far."

Drew nodded. "Mac called your grandparents. They're thrilled to know that you're safe. They want you to call them when you can. I'd do it tonight if I were you. Your grandmother sounds like she could use it." James nodded. "As for us not keeping you here, it's a done deal. We've contacted the right people, and as of now you're our temporary son. But only until we can get it legalized."

"I don't want to...." He started crying, softly at first then harder as he sat there. His words, jumbled and full of emotion, tore at Drew's heart. "She never loved me like.... I tried so hard to be.... I just wanted to be like the rest of them. But no matter how hard.... Why, Mr. Drew? What did I do that was so terrible that she could never love me?"

"I don't know how to answer that for you." James nodded,

his tears still flowing freely. "But your grandparents love you, and Mac and I are going to love you too. We're going to make this work, all right?"

James nodded and leaned back on the chair again. Drew did as well. When Mac came out to join them, bringing cake for the three of them, Drew smiled. He was feeling free for the first time in forever, it felt.

CHAPTER 12

James threw the ball for Rory again. It was amazing to him that something that was done over and over for a dog never seemed to bore him. He was having a good time too. Just not having to worry about anything for a change had him not only sleeping better, but his appetite was back too. He supposed it helped that he had a bed and food whenever he wanted it. Looking up at the house when he heard the door open, he waved at Mac as she brought a dying plant out of the house. He'd seen three of these dead or dying things around the house since he'd gotten here.

"You don't have a very green thumb, do you?" She told him that she only had to touch a plant, no matter how healthy it was, and it died. "I love things that grow. Can I see if I can save it?"

"Have at it. And while you're at it, there are two more that are going to die soon too. I have no idea if I'm overwatering them or not giving them enough." He looked at the saturated dirt and told her she'd overwatered it. "Doesn't matter. It'll be dead in a week if I have to care for it. I can plant things in the yard and have them grow. Not greatly, mind you, but they do survive me. Maybe it's the guy who mows for me. I have no idea."

As he dumped some of the water out of the pot, he heard the woman next door screaming at the top of her lungs. She'd been doing that a lot lately. Yelling across the yards like she had to make sure that the world knew she was around. James looked at Mac when she huffed. The neighbor was talking even as she came through the gate and toward the two of them.

"Mac, if you don't curb that dog, I'm going to have the police come out here and shoot him." James wanted to tell her that if she did that he'd shoot her back, but said nothing when Mac stepped off the deck. This was going to be epic, he just knew it. As he put the plant behind him on the floor for safekeeping, he whistled for Rory to come to him.

"You go ahead and call them, Olivia. And while you're at it, you should let them know that you might be moving out soon. It might be healthier for you if you did anyway. You're starting to really piss me off." Olivia asked her what the hell she was talking about. "Oh, you didn't hear? I bought out the people around you. They were only too happy to sell. Seems you'd made an enemy or two in the last few weeks, and they were glad to have the last laugh. Even the two lots that you claimed were yours all these years. Nasty of you to do that to the Millers, don't you think? Take their land when you had no rights to it?"

"I have no idea what you mean. But just so you know, I'm going to own your land too, see if I don't. I own that lot and the one on the other side of me too." Mac only shook her head. "You can't do that. I had it in writing that it belonged to me."

"Funny thing about that. No one has any record of that little bit of paperwork you claim to have. I even had my attorney search out the tax records on it. Did you know that no one has paid them in ten years? Isn't that about the time you moved into this area?" Olivia took a step toward them, doubling up her fist as she did. Mac moved in her direction, stepping between Olivia and him. "You touch him or me and it will be over before you get your hand back. If you do."

He saw it then. It was an emotion that he was very familiar with. Fear. Olivia was afraid of Mac. James felt himself stand up taller, his body felt stronger. She had stood up to the woman for him so that she'd not hit him. James fell in love with the strong woman.

"You can't threaten me. I'm a well-respected woman around here." James couldn't help it, he snorted. Olivia looked at him like she was going to hit him, and he felt his body tense for the pain. But before anything happened, Drew had the woman turned and her arm jerked up behind her back. James had never even seen him come out of the house, much less move.

"You have overstayed your welcome, Olivia. I think you should go on home before you get your arm broken and your face busted up. I've had a really great morning so far, and you are not going to fuck it up." He gave her a small shove and let her go. When she staggered away from him, James was sure it was over until she turned around. The gun startled him to the point where he couldn't move.

The report of the gun was loud. And when he fell backwards, thinking that he was a dead kid, James waited for the hurt. He knew as surely as he was laying there that Olivia had killed him when he'd just found happiness. But as he lay there, his body weighed down by something, he heard screams and yelling and had to move Rory off him to sit up. He was surprised to find nothing hurt.

Olivia was now on the ground, her arms pulled up tightly behind her back again and her mouth bloody. Drew held her

175

down like he meant business, his face calm but hard. Mac was on the phone, talking calmly to whoever was on the other end. Then he realized that Drew was talking to him. It took him several seconds to realize he was asking him if he was all right.

"Yes, sir." He felt his body, his hands moving up and down his chest and arms, and didn't feel any places that he might have been sprouting blood, and nodded again. "I'm all right so far as I can see. I guess she missed me."

Drew only nodded, his eyes on the wall above his head. James turned and looked at the shattered glass of the sliding door as well as the neat hole in the middle of it. Glass was just behind him, broken in so many pieces that James had the sudden urge to reach out and see if it was ice. Then he looked at the door again.

Standing up, he realized it was right about where his heart would have been had he been.... James looked at Rory, who was watching him carefully.

"He knocked you down. I didn't even have time to react before Rory had you down and Drew was taking care of Olivia." James heard the words coming out of Mac's mouth, but they didn't seem to be making any sense whatsoever. "James, you should probably sit down now. You're looking quite white."

"Yes, ma'am." Sitting was easy. His knees were weak and he was sure that every bone in his body was shaking too. As he reached for the table to hold him steady, Rory came and put his head on his knee. It felt to James like he was telling him he had this now. He'd be fine. "You saved me, didn't you boy?"

Rory yipped, a sound that said, *yes I did, you silly human.* As they sat there, James petting the dog and being ever so grateful for the chance to do so, he heard sirens as they came screaming up the road. He'd been in this house for less than twenty-four hours and someone had tried to kill him. But James had never felt so safe in his entire life. Smiling for the first time in a very long while, James knew he was going to be all right.

The police took Olivia away, her kicking and screaming the whole time. Olivia tried to tell them that they had forced her hand, and had not played fairly with her. As she was being put in the back seat of the car, she screamed some very colorful names at Mac that he'd heard his mom call him. Olivia also called him a few names. But it didn't bother him at all. He'd been called worse. But the best part of the interview with the police was when Mac came in and put her arm around his shoulders, asking him if he needed anything. He'd been so emotional that all he'd been able to do was shake his head.

"Mrs. Dutch said that you've been harassing her for days now." Before he could tell the police officer that he'd only arrived here last night, she winked at him. "We don't believe her. She told us a week ago that Mr. Miller was peeking in her bedroom window. He's ninety years old and uses a walker to get around. And her bedroom is on the second floor. Unless he knows something we don't, we just wrote her off."

"She's been harassing my family." He smiled. It had been the first time he'd used that term too. "I don't know all of it, but she came over here and started telling us that the dog was bothering her. And that she was going to shoot him. Rory is a good dog, and the yard is fenced in."

"We've had dealings with her before, as I said." She took notes before looking up at him. "I know your parents, James. And I'm really glad that you're here with a good family. I've known Mac for almost my entire life. She's the best there is."

"Her and Drew said I'd be safe here." The officer nodded and patted his hand. "My grandparents are coming by to see me later in the week. I hope that my...I hope my mom and stepfather don't find out. They threatened to not let them see my little brother if they did that."

"You have any trouble with them, you call me. Day or night." She handed him a business card after writing a number on the back. "That's my home number, and on the front is my work one. I'll leave word at the desk that they're to contact me if you call in. I'll make sure that nothing goes badly for you. Like I said, you're with good people now, and they'll make sure you're all right."

After the police left, Mac went to her office to make some calls. James went out on the deck again and played with the dog. When Mac was finished they were going into Extreme and he was going to start working off his debt. He and Drew had made out a payment plan, and he felt really good about it all. Then tomorrow they were going shopping. James already had more new clothes in his room than he'd had since he'd lived with his stepfather. Plus there was a new computer and printer, a stereo that he'd read up on last night on how to use it, and his own bathroom. He wondered how he'd been so lucky.

~~~

Drew watched the men working. As of yesterday the land around them, all three hundred acres, was theirs. Even the bitch Olivia had sold them her little plot of land when it was apparent that she wasn't going to be able to move forward with her plans of running him and Mac off, and that she might need the money for court costs. And of course, Mac had told her that they'd not press charges if she sold it to them cheap. He thought they got a good price on it.

178

"The barn and the shelter house are looking good, don't you think?" Hugh sat next to him on the deck that was being extended as well. "I mean, when you guys said it was going to start immediately, you weren't kidding. I even like how you're blending in the new bedrooms with the house you have. You will have the biggest residential log cabin in the world at this rate."

"Mac knows a lot of people around here, and they want this to work as well." He didn't add that Steele and the rest of the group had also backed them, and they now had three crews working on the different projects to get them done before winter set in. "Becky comes home the day after tomorrow. James has been helping out with getting her room ready. I'm hoping she likes it."

"What little girl wouldn't?" He had no idea but Hugh just laughed at him. "Are you ready for this? The reason I ask is, you seem to be. But I've known you a long time, and one thing I will never do is play poker with you. You have a very unreadable face. But I will say, my friend, that I've never seen you look so relaxed before. Married life seems to agree with you on all kinds of levels."

"I do feel really good, as a matter of fact. And I'm not sure it's married life or just being at peace with a great many personal things. My mother being one of them." Hugh just nodded at him. "I think I'm ready for this phase in my life as well. I don't know a great deal about kids, but I think the two we have so far are pretty amazing. James is ready for school to start in a couple of weeks. And he goes in next week to get tested for grade placement and such. Becky will require a little extra work on our part in that she needs to go to therapy a lot these next few weeks, but she will be walking soon, so that'll help. There are some hiccups that we've encountered, but those are minor compared to what they might have been."

"Like what?" Drew told him. "Minor, yes those are, but taken care of too. I don't think that the grandparents wanting him to stay with them a couple of weekends a month will be too bad. And it'll give you and Mac a break too. You can learn how to do most anything put before you, Drew. So I'd not worry too much about how you're going to help Mac out in the business. She seems to have a pretty good head on her shoulders anyway. And James won't tell anyone about what you guys are if that has you worried. I mean, being immortal will come out sometime, but if you play it right, no one will care. As for Kari and her being a cat, he didn't freak out, did he?"

"No. He took it pretty well. Vinnie scares him. But let's face it, she scares us all a little." Hugh laughed again. "And Alexandra has him calling her Grandma, so that's working out. And little Aster thinks he's the greatest person in the world. You should see the two of them together. I think that she'd live with us too just to be with James. He's a really great kid."

Addie was due soon, and three weeks later Dillon was due as well. They looked hot and miserable, but he'd learned the hard way not to point out that they might look like they were going to explode. Addie was especially sensitive about her size. Dillon threatened to shoot the next person that asked her how she was feeling, and in general, the men just watched them and kept their mouths shut. Mac, however, just told them to shut up and sit down, which they did.

"Your house back home, I've got a buyer for it if you want to sell." He told Hugh that he had no use for it. "Good. The city is looking for a place to change over to some kind of high roller hotel. It would only cater to a few people. Six, I think.

But that's been put on hold. I think that Steele is going to buy it if they don't make a decision within the next few weeks, I think by Thanksgiving. If you want to really sell, then I'd say wait a few weeks, then sell to Steele. He'll pay you quick, and there won't be the red tape involved with the city buying it."

"Whatever he wants. I'd much prefer to sell it to him anyway. Will he convert it to that, you think?" Hugh told him that was the plan. "That'll be good for the area. I heard that Vinnie has more business than she can handle most days, and that there are people from all over the world coming to see what she has."

Vinnie had a beautiful antique store that catered to the rich. There were some very high priced items along with some smaller ones in the store, as well as jewelry that hadn't seen the light of day for decades. Most of it had come from a vampire that she knew a long time ago, but she was getting more and more business all the time from a lot more of them. Vampires wanting to get rid of things that they might have had for centuries and had no more use for.

"The donations for this home we're working on, you should hear how much we have already. I think Steele has made it his personal business to make sure that we're well funded for the rest of our lives…well, forever I guess." Hugh told him that he'd contributed as well. "Thank you very much. I think that this will be as good for us as it will be for the kids. I'm looking forward to seeing how we get it working."

"How many kids are you going to take at a time? I know that Anna, your cook, has come to help you out here, but how many are you going to see if you can help?" Drew had no idea and said that to him. "I'm to understand that the addition to your house, the dorm rooms, it can hold up to a dozen kids. You thinking of hiring out some help with that?"

"Are you looking for a job?" Hugh told him he was fine where he was for now. Like him, Hugh had gotten burnt out at helping ghosts. But he told Drew that he was going to stick it out until something better came along. "We're interviewing for six adults to help us out. And Vinnie is going to have a few of the vamps that she knows come and work the night shift. She said that they're needing a better gig. Whatever that means."

He'd talked to her last night. Well, he and Mac had. She'd told him that the vamps she had in mind were older, didn't need anything other than something to look forward to, and they didn't feed as much as they had long ago, so they wouldn't have to leave the kids to go and take care of that often. Mac had told her that the kids wouldn't be lunch, and Vinnie told her she'd kill anyone who tried that. Drew was pretty sure she meant that literally, not just as an idle threat.

"What I'd like to do, if you don't mind, is come out here sometimes. Not just to help out, but to work at what Mac and you have to offer with the Extreme business. I think...I need to get out more, and maybe on my weeks off, I could come out, learn how to be a guide on a couple of things, and work out that way. I need to be around more people that are living and breathing before I eat a bullet." Drew didn't ask him if he was serious. One thing about Hugh that he'd learned a long time ago, the man was one step away from ending it all every day. He was depressed. He hid it well, but he was depressed all the same. "I'm sure you can find a thing or two for me to do, can't you?"

"Yes." Not a hesitation in his answer either. He was his friend and would be for life. "You come out any time you want. We'll find something. You might want to hurt us when you have to deal with some of the people that come through, but you always have a job and a place to stay when you need us."

"I'm going to purchase a house here. Not on this part of the river, but nearby. Some place I can come and just chill if I want." That worried Drew, but he didn't voice it. But Hugh seemed to know. "I won't leave my body for you to find, Drew. I swear to you. When I go, it'll be quick and no one will ever find my body. You know the drill when I come up missing."

He did too. There were people to notify if he was gone for more than a week, and more people if it was a month. Then after a year, he'd told Drew to cut his losses, he was dead, and to file for the insurance. Everything was in his name, including his homes. Drew had done the same for him when they'd both been single.

As they sat there and talked about nothing at all, Drew thought of his life now. There were ghosts here…most of them just came and went as if they knew who he was but didn't care. There were two that he'd have to keep his eye on…they just looked like trouble. But for the most part, it was quiet here. He knew that once spring and summer rolled around it would be different, but for now, he loved his new life and home.

After Hugh left, with the promise that he'd come back for dinner, Drew went into the house. James had gone into Extreme with Mac to meet a few of the crew that would stay on until after the holiday and to pick up some dinner. Drew had elected to stay behind and wait on the boxes that were being delivered today with some of the equipment for the new barn. Making his way out to the smaller, older barn, he saw the man before the man saw him. But when he turned, Drew saw it was a woman, not a man.

The way she was dressed, baggy shirt and pants, had him

thinking she was dressed this way because she was hiding out, not that it was the way she preferred to dress. Boots that were opened and unlaced looked completely out of place with the delicate soft features of her face. Her hair was up under a too large hat; the bits of it hanging from under it were light, almost silver he thought in the darkness of the barn. And she had a haunted look in her eyes, dark eyes that looked much older than he'd bet she was.

"Hello." She nodded but didn't move. He could see that she was too thin, but she was clean, and he also noticed that her way of dress wasn't going to make it now that the nights were colder. "Do you need someone? Mac, maybe?"

"No." Drew didn't go further into the barn. Not that he was afraid of her, but she might be bait for someone hiding in the shadows. "I came to see if I could have some food. Or an old blanket if you have one."

"Come up to the house and I'll feed you." He knew it was stupid, she could be a mass murderer or something, but he suddenly trusted her. "There's a room you can use too, and a shower and a bed if you want."

"No thanks. Just some food and a blanket. And if it's all the same to you, I'd just as soon not go in your house. I don't know you, now do I?" Good point, he told her. "The woman next door, Dutch, she's gone, right? That woman would make the most sainted man curse up a storm on his best days, don't you think?"

"Yes. She's been arrested. And she's sold out and is awaiting trial, I guess. She won't be coming back any time too soon, I don't think. Did you need something from her? Or were you related somehow?" The woman shook her head but didn't elaborate. "I'm Drew Mullins. My wife is Mac, and our children are Becky and James."

184

"I know." She didn't offer up her name and he had to smile. She was a cautious little thing. Not that he blamed her, but it was a little funny. "Food?"

"Oh yeah." As he moved back to the house, he thought about being immortal. It was a strange thought, but with her at his back he wanted to make sure that if she had a gun, he didn't die trying to help her. He was going to have to talk to someone about that. He had no idea if that meant he couldn't ever be killed no matter what, or there were guidelines. Asking her to have a seat on the deck, he went inside to ask Anna if she had something hot and quick for someone.

"That girl?" He nodded, wondering how she knew about her so quickly. "I got some blankets too that I'll give her. You stay on in here and I'll take care of her. You're a mite big and could be scaring her."

He started to tell her she hadn't been afraid of him in the barn but closed his mouth. Anna already thought he was weird, he didn't want to add to it. Watching from the window, he could see that she wasn't having any more luck with the girl than he had. But she did start eating after she was left on her own. He watched the woman carefully, looking for clues as to why she was out in the barn and who she was. Or, he supposed, what she was.

The blankets were taken out and laid on the chair next to her, but neither the girl nor Anna spoke that time. Ten minutes later, both the girl and the blankets were gone.

"She'll be back." Drew nodded, wondering if she'd really ever left. "I'll start having things around that she can take with her that are nutritious and such."

"And some fruit. I'll make sure that there is bottled water out there as well all the time. There's an old refrigerator that we can fill up with it so she can stay hydrated as well."

Anna patted him on the cheek as she moved by him. Drew couldn't remember anyone ever doing that before and liked it. Whistling, he made his way out to the barn to prepare for the girl, taking some more blankets that had arrived for the new addition with him.

By the time Mac returned, leaving James at the shop to work, he had the barn cleaned up, the fridge on, and the water that he'd had in the house put inside. When she came out to ask him what he was up to, it was fun telling her what he and Anna had done.

"Her name is Peach. I'm not sure if that's what it really is, but that's what she told me when I cornered her one night about six months ago. To be honest with you, I never thought of her again after that." Drew told her how he'd had Anna feed her. "She's been around for a while. I don't know her story or anything. You think that she's homeless?"

"I think she's something. What I mean is, I have a feeling that she's not quite human. I have no idea what, but she's more than likely a shifter." Mac asked him how he knew. "Kari said there are signs that you can see if you look. Movements of her hands. The way she tilts her head to hear something far away. Like I said, she might just be human, but I don't think so."

After leaving the barn unlocked, the two of them went to the house. It was going to be a long day tomorrow, getting the boating part of the business closed up for the winter months and getting the mountain climbing ready for the die-hard campers that came around. Drew had no idea that there were so many things a person could do in the winter months to keep in shape.

By the time James was dropped off a little before six, dinner was about ready and the four of them, Anna included, sat down to eat. Things, Drew knew, could change in a second in a person's life, and he wanted to make sure that they all sat down together at least once a day.

Before You Go...

HELP AN AUTHOR

write a review

THANK YOU!

Share your voice and help guide other readers to these wonderful books. Even if it's only a line or two your reviews help readers discover the author's books so they can continue creating stories that you'll love. Login to your favorite retailer and leave a review. Thank you.

Kathi Barton, winner of the Pinnacle Book Achievement award as well as a best-selling author on Amazon and All Romance books, lives in Nashport, Ohio with her husband Paul. When not creating new worlds and romance, Kathi and her husband enjoy camping and going to auctions. She can also be seen at county fairs with her husband who is an artist and potter.

Her muse, a cross between Jimmy Stewart and Hugh Jackman, brings her stories to life for her readers in a way that has them coming back time and again for more. Her favorite genre is paranormal romance with a great deal of spice. You can visit Kathi on line and drop her an email if you'd like. She loves hearing from her fans. aaronskiss@gmail.com.

Follow Kathi on her blog: http://kathisbartonauthor.blogspot.com/

www.ingramcontent.com/pod-product-compliance
Lightning Source LLC
Chambersburg PA
CBHW032139170626
46808CB00006B/2300